BLOW FOR BLOW

Big Mike shot out one enormous fist and punched Fargo square in the chest. It knocked him back five feet, and he landed on his ass.

As he struggled to get some air back into his lungs, he heard Mike laugh like a braying donkey, and the woman, Cally, shouting, "Mike, you big, dumb brute! He was just standin' there!"

Fargo finally caught his breath, and struggled to his feet. The woozy feeling he'd had from the beer was long gone, replaced by adrenaline. But his judgement still wasn't exactly the best, because he put his head down like a bull and charged Mike, full tilt.

He butted the son of a bitch right in the belly, and he must have taken him completely by surprise, because this time it was Mike who flew backward and landed on his backside.

You're in for it now, Fargo thought belatedly.

THE TRAILSMAN

#271

ST. LOUIS SINNERS

by

Jon Sharpe

A SIGNET BOOK

SIGNET
Published by New American Library, a division of
Penguin Group (USA) Inc., 375 Hudson Street,
New York, New York 10014, U.S.A.
Penguin Books Ltd, 80 Strand,
London WC2R 0RL, England
Penguin Books Australia Ltd, 250 Camberwell Road,
Camberwell, Victoria 3124, Australia
Penguin Books Canada Ltd, 10 Alcorn Avenue,
Toronto, Ontario, Canada M4V 3B2
Penguin Books (N.Z.) Ltd, Cnr Rosedale and Airborne Roads,
Albany, Auckland 1310, New Zealand

Penguin Books Ltd, Registered Offices:
80 Strand, London WC2R 0RL, England

First published by Signet, an imprint of New American Library,
a division of Penguin Group (USA) Inc.

First Printing, May 2004
10 9 8 7 6 5 4 3 2 1

The first chapter of this book originally appeared in *Colorado Corpse,* the
two hundred seventieth volume in this series.

The Trailsman

Beginnings . . . they bend the tree and they mark the man. Skye Fargo was born when he was eighteen. Terror was his midwife, vengeance his first cry. Killing spawned Skye Fargo, ruthless, cold-blooded murder. Out of the acrid smoke of gunpowder still hanging in the air, he rose, cried out a promise never forgotten.

The Trailsman they began to call him all across the West: searcher, scout, hunter, the man who could see where others only looked, his skills for hire but not his soul, the man who lived each day to the fullest, yet trailed each tomorrow. Skye Fargo, the Trailsman, the seeker who could take the wildness of a land and the wanting of a woman and make them his own.

St. Louis, 1860—
The sins of the father may be visited upon the son,
but the child who walks alone is threatened with
damnation at every turn—where salvation's last
hope lies on the cold end of a smoking gun.

1

It had been a long, tough search.

Not long in days, maybe, but what he was looking for was as tough to find as a moose in a henhouse. So he'd decided on a little rest and recreation, in the form of one Miss Lola—she never gave her last name—in the employ of Dustin's Red Dog saloon, just on the outskirts of St. Louis.

Lola took him upstairs and stripped out of that little red dress as quick as if it were buttered, and had him out of his britches just as quickly.

He might have wished for a little more lead-in time just to set the mood, so to speak, but Lola was in a hurry.

"Got an eleven o'clock regular," she confided as she eased herself down on him.

Woman on top was a novelty for Fargo, but in this case, it was fine with him. She moved like a bronc rider up there, slick and hot and wide-eyed and wild, but not too wild.

He bucked up into her, once he caught her rhythm, and pretty soon those eyes of hers closed and her mouth opened, and she was taking in air in little gasps and gulps, and making tiny sounds of surprise and pleasure deep in her throat.

Her round, honey breasts danced with her movements and shuddered with his, their salmon-colored nipples tightening and darkening, twisting into hard little knots of flesh, which he reached up and grabbed, gently plucking and pulling at them.

She let out a quivering little "Ahhhh!" when he touched her, as if she were unaccustomed to such caresses, and craned her neck back.

Fargo felt himself building, building, building, and then, with a cry that shook even him, Lola came in a great burst of pleasure. As she did, her inner muscles tightened on Fargo, shoving him over the edge and into the abyss. He felt himself tumbling and tumbling and tumbling, and finally opened his eyes to find Lola collapsed on his chest.

Christ!

She was panting hard, and whispered, "You're gonna stick around, ain't you, cowboy? I swear to Jesus, iff'n you do, it's on the house from now on. I ain't never, I mean, not since I was a kid of seventeen . . ."

He rolled them both over, so that they were lying side by side. He stroked damp hair away from her face. It was a nice enough face, not beautiful, but not plain either. And she had the cutest spray of freckles, right across her upturned nose.

Right now, her expression was pure, unadulterated bliss. And he'd put it there.

"Sorry, Lola," he said, smiling. "Just passin' through. But if I ever come this way again, I'll keep your offer in mind."

She kissed his temple, then sat up. "Just my luck," she said with a shake of her head. "First fella in years that's made me see the elephant, and he's movin' on."

She sighed, then reluctantly stood up and began to gather her clothes.

Fargo grabbed his britches up off the floor. He'd counted on a little more time to lie there and bask, and maybe a tad *more* time for another go-round. But then, Lola had that eleven o'clock regular, and after all, he was only passing through.

Fargo got up and pulled his britches on, while Lola wandered over to the window. Lacing up her blouse, she said, "Didn't you ride in here on that big paint horse?"

"I did," said Fargo. He gave a last tug to his britches. "Well, looks like somebody's tryin' to make off with him."

It was bright outside. Fargo walked out the swinging doors of Dustin's Red Dog saloon, only to find a fifteen-year-old kid hanging on to the Ovaro's reins and tugging with all his might.

Now, Fargo knew damn well that the Ovaro wouldn't go off with anybody but him—and Fargo also had a few beers in him and had been into Lola, so to speak, which in this case heightened his sense of humor—so he just leaned up against the building and watched for a second.

The kid pulled and pulled, trying to get the black and white paint stallion to take even one step, but he might as well have been trying to haul off Pike's Peak with a lasso made of thread. The Ovaro just stood there stubbornly at the rail and snorted calmly, whiffling his nostrils.

The kid tugged and pulled and swore, then hauled on the reins some more, but no dice.

Finally, Fargo couldn't keep his mouth shut any longer. He said, "Having some trouble, son?"

The boy, tallish, dark-haired, and owning the promise of growing up into a quite handsome fellow—if he didn't get hanged for horse theft first—said, "It's this damn horse, Mister. Can't get the son of a bitch to budge!" To the Ovaro, the boy said, "C'mon, Charlie, old boy! Get a move on!"

The kid was a good liar. Fargo would give him that. Why, if he didn't know different, he would've believed that the Ovaro belonged to the kid.

Fargo said, "Well, why don't you hop up on him? Ride him out. Maybe he just doesn't want to be led."

And then, biting his cheek, he waited for the festivities to begin.

"That's an idea, Mister," the oblivious boy said

gratefully. "Don't know why I didn't just do that in the first damn place."

Settling his too-big hat on his head, the kid slung the Ovaro's reins around the horse's neck, took hold of a handful of mane, and slid his foot into the stirrup. He was almost in the saddle when the Ovaro put his head down and bucked out his hind quarters big, but just once, throwing the boy flying.

In fact, the kid landed on his ass in the middle of the street, narrowly missing a passing buggy.

Fargo stifled a chuckle and asked, with as straight a face as he could muster, "Say, that stud's rank! You all right, kid?"

The boy stood up, shaking his limbs and checking for damage, and shouted. "Reckon so. I just don't know what's got into old Sunny."

"Thought you said his name was Charlie," Fargo replied.

"Sunny Charlie," the boy said, covering quickly. He dusted his britches off. "My ma named him." He said those four words as if they explained everything, and Fargo nodded.

The boy came back over to the Ovaro and stood there a moment, just looking at him. If he'd made a move to hurt the horse in any way, shape, or form, Fargo was ready to jump on him and pound him into the ground. For now, though, he was just willing to wait and see.

But the kid only patted the Ovaro on his neck and gave him an admiring look. He whispered something to the horse that Fargo couldn't hear, and then he looped the stallion's reins over the hitching rail again. He had given up, it looked like.

"What's your name, kid?" Fargo asked casually as he slowly stood erect.

"Toby," the boy said. "And I ain't a kid. I'm fifteen. Almost sixteen."

Well, Fargo hadn't been off on his age.

He said, "Fair enough, Toby. You gonna leave old, uh, Sunny Charlie just tied up? It's gettin' kind of

4

hot out here." He glanced up at the sun, which was directly overhead.

Toby shrugged. "I guess my pa will have to come get him. He can be a stubborn cuss."

Fargo grinned. "Your pa or your horse?"

Toby gave out sort of a lopsided grin. "Both?"

Fargo took a couple of steps forward, and stepped down off the walk, right next to the Ovaro's head. "Well, Toby, you are one crackerjack of a fast thinker. And a good straight-faced liar."

Toby's face wadded up with indignation. "Hey! Who you callin' a liar, Mister?"

Fargo unwrapped the Ovaro's reins from the rail, then ducked under it, coming face to face with Toby.

"You, son," Fargo said conversationally.

Toby backed up a step, but backed right into the buckskin that was tied next to the Ovaro.

"Don't go runnin' off," Fargo said. Then he turned to the Ovaro and said, "Back."

The horse backed up until he was clear of the other mounts, then stopped, his head nodding, his reins dangling free.

Realization crossed Toby's face and stayed there, along with a good shot of panic. "Shit!" he muttered, and tried to duck under the buckskin's neck to make a break for it.

But Fargo was too fast for him. He grabbed the boy by his ragged shirt and hauled him back.

"Whoa up! Not so fast, there," he said. "How would you like a job, Toby?"

The boy's face went through a rapid series of changes, but finally settled on disbelief. "What?" he said. "You escape from some looney bin? You're crazier than I am!"

But Fargo just laughed at him. He did, indeed, have a little job for a boy who was quick in his mind and on his feet, and Toby had happened along at just the right time. He'd found the moose in the henhouse, or so he hoped.

"Nope," Fargo said in all sincerity. "I'm not crazy,

and I do have a job for you. If you can manage to be honest for a week. Just with me, though. The pay's two hundred and fifty bucks."

This time, Toby's eyes grew round as proverbial saucers. "You're connin' me, that's what you're doin'!" he said, but Fargo could tell there was something in him that wanted to believe.

"No con," Fargo said. "Now, you look like you haven't eaten in a week and a half. What do you say we take the Ovaro, here, down to the livery, and then I'll take you to lunch. My treat."

At this, the first mention of the Ovaro's name, Toby cocked his head. "The *Ovaro*?" He blinked a couple of times. "Hey, what's your name, Mister?"

"Fargo," came the answer. "Skye Fargo."

"Shit!" the boy yelped, and pulled one of those damned nickel books out of his back pocket. Fargo cringed. The boy unfolded it and excitedly pointed a finger at the figure on the cover.

"Hot damn!" he cried. "You're real? The beard, the bucks, the Ovaro . . . I should'a knowed you right off. Holy Hannah, the one and only Trailsman, right here in Dustin!"

"Better close your mouth before flies start layin' eggs in it, Toby," Fargo said, and started down the street. The big stallion, his reins still dangling, followed him like a giant black and white puppy dog.

Toby did much the same.

2

What had started it began a few days earlier.

The Trailsman had been seated in a wide armchair in Armstrong Leery's dark, sandalwood-scented library. Outside the velvet-draped windows, the distant but bustling St. Louis street traffic moved along.

"Sorry, can't do it," he'd said to Armstrong as he accepted an expensive Havana from the offered box. He ran it under his nose. It smelled of Cuba and dark, sleek girlish thighs and sweat, as well as rich tobacco soaked in brandy.

He smiled.

Armstrong, his friend of almost ten years, furrowed a brow now touched with silver. "Why not, Fargo?" he asked, and his tone was almost hurt, almost bruised. "You can do it if anybody can, my friend. I trust you. If five hundred isn't enough, I'll pay anything you want. The police are damned useless! And besides, I know no other man besides you who can be so devious yet so honest."

Again, Fargo smiled. "You have a way of talking folks into things, Armstrong," he allowed as he pulled a lucifer from the little jar on the desk.

"But I don't know," he went on. "Couldn't promise anything. This man Dawber must be one tough bird if he operated under the nose of the Chicago Police Department for ten years before they managed to

7

track him down and corner him. And even then, you tell me that he gave them the slip!"

Fargo shook his head. "And now he's been working here in St. Louis for three years. There's no way I could find him and get your ring back if the St. Louis constabulary know he's here, but can't find him. And besides, from what you tell me, you need a kid for this. Somebody real innocent looking, baby-faced. And that's not me on any account."

With a sigh, Fargo bit off the end of his cigar, then struck the match on the bottom of his boot.

"If such a person exists," Armstrong said quietly, "then you're the man who can find him. And train him, if need be."

Armstrong leaned forward, elbows on the desk, hands flat out in an plea. "Please, Fargo. Please try. I must have it back. It's priceless! At least we know he hasn't sold it. The police have been able to determine that much."

Fargo exhaled a clean white plume of sweet smoke, laced with the enticing taste of brandy. He leaned back. Dammit, he knew he couldn't do any good for Armstrong. But the man looked absolutely pitiful. Armstrong's strong, craggy face and pitiful didn't go together one whit.

"All right," Fargo said at last, with a deep sigh. "You're goddamn convincing. I'll try." But then he added, "But I'm not promising anything!"

"That's good enough for me, Fargo," Armstrong said, and smiled in what Fargo took for relief. "Fargo's promise to try is better than anyone else's vow to deliver!"

If he'd been Armstrong, he wouldn't have been so quick to relax.

And now, Fargo was seated across the table from Toby—whose last name he'd learned was Jones—at the Gabbling Goose Café, in a little town called Dustin on the outskirts of St. Louis.

"Just what is it you want me to do, Fargo?" Toby

was asking, and he didn't bother to hide his suspicion. He looked, in fact, like he was ready to bolt.

"Got to ask you a few questions, first, kid," Fargo said, and signaled for the waiter. "Like, are you hungry?"

"Course I'm hungry!" Toby said. "And you already asked."

"That I did," said Fargo as the waiter stepped up to their table. He offered two pasteboard menus, which Fargo turned down with a wave of his hand.

"We'll have two steaks," Fargo said, "big ones, and sirloin. Fried potatoes, corn, peas, applesauce, coffee . . ."

He looked over at Toby, who was almost drooling. ". . . and a big glass of milk. We'll order dessert after. Make my steak rare." He looked over at Toby.

"Oh!" the boy said, as if he were coming out of shock. "Medium, please."

The waiter nodded and strode away.

"Criminy," Toby muttered.

Fargo asked, "Problem?"

"You ain't kiddin' with this meal, are you?" Toby asked. "I mean, I ain't had a feed like this since I don't remember."

"Afraid it's going to disappear?" Fargo asked with a smile.

"Afraid it ain't never gonna come," the boy answered, and craned his neck toward the kitchen door.

Fargo grinned. "Don't worry. But you got to do a little earning first, okay?"

Toby sat back in his chair. "Okay. What you wanna know?"

"You got any kin?"

Toby shook his shaggy head. "No, sir. Nobody. Why? You wanna adopt me?"

Fargo laughed. "Hardly. But I want to make sure that you don't take this job and get halfway into it, and that your weepin' mama doesn't show up and blow it all to hell."

Toby snuck a look toward the kitchen door again

before he said, "Told you, I ain't got nobody. My ma died havin' me, and my pa?" He shrugged. "Don't know who he was."

"Who raised you?" Fargo asked. Not that it mattered for the job. He was just curious, that's all.

"A stinkin' orphanage over in Kansas City," the boy said. "They kicked me out when I turned fourteen."

"So you've been on the streets and on your own for almost two years?"

"About the size of it." Toby shot a look back toward the kitchen again. "How long does it take them to sear a steak here, anyhow?"

"Just hold your horses, kid," Fargo said. "They probably got to kill the steer first."

Toby snorted.

Fargo leaned back in his chair and drummed his fingers on the tabletop. "Where you live?"

Toby's jaw muscles worked for a second, and then he said, "What is this anyway, Fargo? How come you wanna know? You gonna come paint my house or something? Sew me some new curtains?"

Fargo leaned back and smiled. "Well, you caught me out, junior. What do you think of a nice celery green?"

Toby scowled. "I live on the street, all right? Ain't had a proper roof since the orphanage. If'n you want to bad enough, you can come paint the alley in back of Grogin's Bar. That's where I been stayin' for the last week."

Fargo gave his fingertips a final drum. "Sorry, kid," he said as he caught sight of their dinners emerging from the kitchen. He supposed he'd have to wait until Toby shoveled in the chow before he got down to any serious business. At least, if he wanted Toby sufficiently sated to hear him out.

He added, "Just trying to figure out your story, that's all."

"Well, that's just about the whole of it," Toby said derisively. But his expression, which had been both pained and bored—and more than a little put out, too—turned on a bottle stopper to one of amazement when the waiter suddenly slid his steak in front of him.

"Criminy!" the boy whispered before, bug-eyed as a hoot owl, he grabbed a fork and dived straight in.

"Here's the deal, kid," Fargo was saying.

And Toby, despite the sleepiness brought on by the best meal he'd had in a coon's age, however long that was, listened.

"My friend, Armstrong Leery," Fargo went on, "has this ring with a great big ruby in it. And when he was wearing it about a week ago, some kids bumped into him on the street. Just kids, he said, kind of dirty lookin', like they hadn't seen soap in a long time."

Toby wondered if that last bit was aimed at him, since he didn't exactly smell like a rose garden, himself, but wisely kept his mouth closed. So far, Fargo was talking about things that had nothing to do with him, so he just listened out of gratitude. After all, it had been an awful good steak.

And he listened out of sheer admiration, too. He couldn't believe his luck, actually bumping into the real, live Fargo, himself!

He touched his pocket and the book in it, and resisted the urge to haul it out and hold it up to Fargo's face to compare the picture to the real man.

"To make a long story short," Fargo continued, oblivious, "the kids got his purse and his ruby ring, and he didn't realize it until after they'd run off."

At this point, Toby broke in. "Say, you're not tryin' to accuse me of that, are you?" he said, Fargo or no. "I may be a lot of things, but I ain't some lowly pickpocket!"

Well, actually, he'd never mastered it. Toby figured that if he tried to lift a man's wallet, the man would have an unbreakable fix on his arm faster than you could say *applesauce*, and he'd likely spend the rest of his life in jail. At least he had some kind of affinity with horses.

Every one of them but Fargo's, that was.

Fargo shook his head and said, "No, nobody's accusing you. Armstrong gave me good description of those kids, and I've been keeping an eye out for them, too. No dice, so far."

Fargo leaned forward slightly, on his elbows, and sent him a serious stare. "I told you there was a job, and there is. The job pays two hundred and fifty, cash money."

Well, the repetition of that sum sure got Toby's attention. He must have straightened right up in his chair, too, because Fargo waved a hand and said, "Down, boy. It's also dangerous. Maybe not as dangerous as trying to mount the Ovaro, but a lot trickier. You think you're up to it?"

Toby shrugged his shoulders, then grinned. "I'm up for anything that pays two-fifty." It seemed a vast fortune to him.

He said, "You want me to find those kids? Fargo, you just tell me what they look like and I'll find you twenty kids that answer the description!"

Fargo snorted, but he smiled. "Not that easy," he said. "The police already found 'em. Course, they lost 'em again . . ."

Toby wrinkled his brow. "Then what do you want me for?"

"To worm your way into their gang," Fargo said—far too casually, Toby thought. "To go to work for their boss. And steal that ruby ring back."

3

He couldn't really tell if the boy trusted him all the way or not, but Fargo was satisfied enough to hand over ten bucks to Toby and send him to the Riverside Hotel. It was a shoddy dive by the riverfront, but it was in the right part of town for their purposes. Toby would be able to find Dawber there.

Or let Dawber find him.

As for Fargo, he was going to a whole different part of town—the Shea Hotel. They didn't have a long ride ahead of them. Dustin, where Fargo had scared up Toby, was only three miles outside of St. Louis, and St. Louis was growing fast enough that Fargo supposed it wouldn't be too many years before Dustin was gobbled up.

But the two didn't travel together. Fargo gave Toby a head start by about fifteen minutes, waiting until Toby hitched a ride with a passing produce wagon before he set out.

Fargo figured they'd best keep separate as much as possible. Dawber had eyes everywhere, if the information he had collected over the past couple of days was correct. The bastard was as slippery as an eel, and just as apt to give a powerful and wholly unexpected jolt to the unfortunate man who actually caught up with him.

Dawber was not only eel-slippery, but just as slimy as one, too, Fargo had learned. Any man who made his living off the backs of homeless boys was scraping the bottom of the bucket. Dawber had a regular force of them, out picking pockets and swiping whatever they could lay their hands on.

Fargo didn't know how Dawber managed it, but not one of the boys, once they were caught—and eventually, most or them were—would ever give Dawber up. Except for that one thirteen-year-old boy, up in Chicago, whose tearful confession had run Dawber to the south, landing him in St. Louis.

Rumor had it that the kid in question had turned up dead a while later. Turned up dead in a back alley, with his hands chopped off.

The whole thing made Fargo sick to his stomach.

The police knew Dawber was in St. Louis, but could never find him. He tended to confine himself to the slums and ghettos of these big, sprawling cities, still rough and tumble in their state of the "old" mixed with rapidly growing new. He lost himself in the warrens of their factory districts and their abandoned buildings, trained his street urchins to be a whole new generation of criminals, and lived off them until they were caught or grew too old for his purposes.

At which point, he just schooled another. And another. And another. He'd been schooling them for a long time, now.

According to Fargo's best estimate, Dawber ran ten to fifteen of the little thieves at a time.

Now, Toby was a bit on the older side for Dawber, and Fargo knew it.

"Tell him you're fourteen, if he asks," he had cautioned the boy. "And slouch."

But he couldn't really countenance sending in a younger kid. Hell, he was still fighting with himself over putting Toby in danger!

But Toby had given him all the right answers. He was on his own, and he'd been on his own for two years. He was enough of a man to make his own decisions, and he had leapt at the chance Fargo offered like a flea leaps on a passing dog.

Of course, Toby could be up there somewhere, jumping on a passing stage with the change from the ten bucks Fargo had laid on him. He could be headed for Illinois or Iowa or Timbuktu, as far as Fargo actually knew.

But he honestly didn't think Toby would run off. In his heart, he couldn't imagine any boy Toby's age turning down a chance to make two hundred and fifty dollars.

It was enough to buy a small house in town or a few acres of nice farmland outside it, or to set himself up in a little business. For many a hardworking man, it was close to two years' salary.

So he really expected Toby to hie himself straight to the Riverside Hotel, and then out onto the streets to start rubbing shoulders with the local kids.

He clucked to the Ovaro, urging him into a soft jog, and headed toward the horizon. The smoke and soot and yellowed sky that hung over St. Louis most days was in sight, like a sick and stationary cloud.

Sighing, Toby sagged down on the edge of what was probably a very buggy bed in his narrow room at the Riverside Hotel.

His window looked out on a brick wall. It didn't much matter. He would have closed it anyway, if it hadn't already been shut tight and painted closed with who knew how many layers of paint. The stench rising from the streets below would have commanded it.

But still, it was a real, honest-to-God luxury to have a bed to sleep on, buggy or not, and a real roof over his head—not to mention walls and a real door that locked from the inside—and for those simple things he was heartily grateful.

He'd thought about just taking off with Fargo's ten dollars. It had sounded mighty tempting, in fact, for a young man who had never had much more than fifty cents in his pocket. But there was such a large carrot out there—two hundred and fifty!—that it made this ten look like birdseed.

Besides, Fargo had sort of intrigued him with the story he'd told about this Dawber character.

And Toby liked feeling, well, needed. Especially when it was by a man as famous as Fargo.

Toby hadn't felt that way for a very long time, if ever. It made him feel kind of important to have somebody counting on him. Like somebody actually knew he was alive. That was sure a change.

Even in the orphanage, none of the grown-ups had even noticed him, save if his desk was vacant in their so-called school or his row wasn't hoed in the field or his bed wasn't made or he hadn't filled his quota of whatever piecework the Old Man had drummed up for them to do that week.

He'd had a friend there. Bass Owen. Bass used to joke that the Bass stood for "bastard," since that's what most of them were.

And even though they were the same age, Bass had got kicked out a year before Toby. The Lord only knew where he was now. Probably dead or in prison, if Toby listened to what the Old Man was always saying.

Well, not always. Twice. And that was about twice as much as the Old Man—Mr. Bartholomew Stevens, who ran the orphanage—ever spoke about anybody.

Besides all that, Toby wanted to see this ruby ring that Fargo's friend wanted back so badly that he'd pay a wandering boy two hundred and fifty bucks to retrieve it for him.

Hell, he was probably paying Fargo something, too. In any case, it was a lot of money.

Course, the ring had to be worth a lot. Probably more than whatever old Armstrong was paying in total.

It had occurred to Toby that maybe he could just grab this priceless ruby ring—if and when he found it—and just take off and run. It was sure tempting, and it had been his first thought, if you wanted to be honest about it.

But then what would he do with it? If this Dawber fellow couldn't get it fenced, how could he?

Fargo said it hadn't turned up anywhere. That's why

they were going straight to Dawber, after all. Fargo said he probably had a hidden stash of such things, things he couldn't get rid of, clear out here in the West.

Fargo said he was probably waiting, holding them like an old age pension, until he could get back East and sell them.

Toby figured that Fargo was probably right.

Fargo was, well, *Fargo*, after all.

Toby stood up, even though he felt like taking a nap. After that big meal and then the long boring ride on the produce wagon, he was all in.

But there were still a few hours of daylight left. He figured he could go wander around the streets, mayhap pick up a loaf of bread, maybe a bit of meat, and a couple of candles. The hotel didn't supply any, as far as he could see.

And candy. It had been a long time since he'd had penny candy.

And maybe he'd buy himself a real, honest to gosh book, too. He'd never owned one, all to himself. He thought that would be a real grown-up thing to do, to buy a book.

He took his tattered—and stolen—copy of *Fargo: Man of the Plains* from his pocket and smoothed it on the thin coverlet. The picture—as beat up and many-times-folded as it was—did kind of look like the real Fargo, didn't it?

And maybe, just maybe, he'd go buy himself a shot of whiskey, too.

Well, try to, anyhow.

"Cally!"

Big Mike Matthews strode in through the tenement's door, stood beside the battered sofa, and shouted again. "Cally!"

A small, flutey voice answered from the back bedroom. "Coming, Mike." It wasn't a particularly happy voice, but then, he didn't expect it to be. He would have liked a little more enthusiasm, though.

"Hurry up," he called. "Get your ass out on the street, you lazy cow. You can turn a couple before we have to go to meet Dawber. What'd you do, sleep all day again?"

She emerged from the bedroom—a tiny, tired-looking redheaded beauty dressed in a shabby but clean pink frock—and walked toward him down the peeling hallway.

"It isn't like I have nothing else to do, Mike," she said flatly. "Had to do the marketing this morning, and go see about poor Grace Cooper."

Big Mike stood there as she pinned on her hat, then walked past him, just like he was a piece of furniture. "Why you care about that old bitch, anyway?" he snarled.

"Because she's a sick old lady, that's why," Cally said as she walked out onto the sagging stoop. "She needs me. You think I'm going to let her lay there in her own dirt? You think I should just leave her there to starve? She needs somebody to get her meals, somebody to look after her!"

Mike followed her. The street was full of people—full of marks, he liked to think—and noisy. Cally locked the door behind them and dropped the key in her ratty little purse.

Mike growled, "Well, I want you to stop hangin' around that old bat and givin' her stuff. She can die on her own nickel. Spend your extra time workin', if you've got so goddamn much of it."

He paused, then hollered, "And that's a damn silly lookin' bonnet. Where'd you get it? It's stupid lookin', with all them curly feathers and pink doodads."

Cally didn't answer. The little snip merely turned on her heel and walked away from him, down the street toward the Little Cougar Café, where she'd be likely to pick up a customer.

"I said, where'd you get that stupid hat?" Mike shouted after her angrily.

He would have slapped her if she hadn't been walking away so quickly and therefore out of reach.

As it was, rather than expend the energy, he simply reached down, picked up a dried road apple off the street, and lobbed it at her back.

It hit her squarely between the shoulders, and she stopped.

"Very funny," she shouted without turning around. "Very funny, Mike. And I found it, damn it. I found it in the trash down at McGinty's Tavern and cleaned it up a mite."

"Sure you did, you lyin' sewer wench!" he hollered.

She didn't answer. But he thought that when she started walking again, she did it with a little more spring in her step.

Goddamn snippy little bitch.

She'd better step lively if she knew what was good for her.

4

After Fargo got the Ovaro put up and got himself settled in his hotel room, he set out to find himself a new suit of clothes. His bucks were a little out of place in St. Louis.

And besides, he wanted to look like anybody but himself for the next few days. Hadn't Toby recognized him right off?

Silently, he cursed whoever the son of a bitch was who was penning those goddamned novels. They were making him quite a bit more well-known than he had ever wanted to be.

At least to the kiddie crowd.

He turned into Fillmore's Men's Store, and there he bought himself a new outfit—city slicker all the way. He emerged wearing brown pants and brown shoes, a white shirt, a brown and yellow checkered vest, and a brown jacket. He bought a pair of cheap but roomy brown leather boots, and on his head was a brown beaver hat, for good measure.

His bucks were rolled in white paper, and he carried this bundle—which the clerk had gingerly wrapped— under his arm.

The new clothes felt scratchy and uncomfortable and the boots felt worse, but he supposed he could get used to them. For a little while, anyhow. If they were lucky, Toby'd get a line on Dawber quickly, and then everything would go back to normal.

From the clothing store, he hailed a cab and was soon click-clacking his way toward Armstrong's. He figured to report his progress so far.

And hopefully, be asked to stay for dinner.

"Are you joshin' me?" growled the bartender. "Eighteen, my ass! Now, get the hell outta here and don't come back till you're shavin'!"

Toby started to form the word *but*, then closed his mouth. This man wasn't going to see reason. Or at least, Toby's version of it.

Aw, hell, he thought as he went through the batwing barroom doors and out into the noisy street. Maybe he really was a perpetual baby face. He'd tried for a whiskey at least twenty times in the past year, and hadn't gotten one yet.

At this rate, they'd keep throwing him out of saloons until he was forty! He'd probably have grandkids by then, too.

He was looking at the ground and mulling over his extreme bad fortune in this matter as he walked up the street, when suddenly, he ran smack into something. Somebody. Or rather, somebody ran right into him.

Toby fell flat on his ass.

The person he'd collided with—a blond-headed kid, younger than he was—didn't so much as look back, let alone say he was sorry. He just leapt over Toby like he had springs in his shoes and kept on running.

A moment later a red-faced policeman came galloping right after him. He, too, jumped over Toby—although not nearly so gracefully—and just kept on thudding and galumphing after his quarry, blowing his tin whistle to beat the band.

Suddenly, Toby remembered why he was there in the first place. "I wonder . . ." he muttered as he stood up and brushed himself off.

He tried to stare after the two but they were long gone, lost in a swirling sea of bustling and uncaring people.

Cally Teach eased back into the noisy, smokey, ripe-with-body-odors Little Cougar Café, once again cursing the fact that she'd ever set her eyes on Big Mike Matthews. Her last trick had stiffed her, and now she'd have to work longer to make it up. She just hoped she wouldn't be late for the meeting with Dawber, although Dawber's meetings were rarely what that name implied.

Usually, they had a drink (or six) while Big Mike and Dawber cooked up schemes, most of which they never put into practice.

She never had more than one drink, though. And that one was just to make them happy. She was more interested in Dawber's children.

Brats, he called them. His never-ending workforce, his inexhaustible supply of brats.

But they weren't brats, not really. Oh, they were hard, all right. What most of them had been through would make anybody hard.

Losing parents or being cast out by them—she wasn't sure which was worse. Roving the streets, half starved, waiting on a chance to steal a crust of bread from the rubbish heap, these were the children who were Dawber's little mob.

Cally tried, in her own way, to give their lives a little softness, to convince them that not everyone was out to use them, to beat them, to throw them away like so much trash.

When those boys ended up at Dawber's, they'd been through enough hell to make Dawber's offer of a roof and food in exchange for a little "work" seem like paradise. She supposed it had something to do with a boy's need for organization, too. Most boys had it, although they didn't know it, and these poor urchins fit right into Dawber's hierarchy, each assuming his place as if he were made for it.

"Well, hullo, darlin'," said an ugly voice behind her that sliced into her thoughts.

She plastered her best smile across her face, then

turned toward the voice. It matched its owner, but she didn't shrink from the man's gruesome facial scar, nor his rough and smelly clothes, nor his pockmarked cheeks. It was just business as usual.

"Hello, yourself, big man," she said in a come-hither tone, quickly taking stock of the brute's style of dress. "Just off the river?"

"That I am, baby, that I am," he said, and in a poor attempt to be suave, added, "Can I get you a mug'a suds, pretty lady? Whiskey maybe?"

He shifted uncomfortably from foot to foot, as if even that small effort to be civil was playing with his patience.

She smiled at him. After living with Big Mike for these past four years, she had learned to force a smile under any set of circumstances.

"Would you rather we just got on with it, honey?" she asked.

The lout looked relieved. They usually did. "Aye," he said. "Alley out back all right?"

"Fine," she said, letting him take her arm. "But you pay first. I ain't gonna get stiffed again."

A surly look passed over his already dark features, but he dug a thick, grimy hand into his pocket, grumbling, "I don't want nothin' fancy and I'm a worldly man. You understand me, Missy?"

She nodded. "Sure."

He nodded right back at her. "How much?"

"You think this boy can actually do us some good?" Armstrong asked over his asparagus and hollandaise.

Fargo paused, a bite of steak—and very good steak, too—poised inches from his lips. He said, "That's a real good question. The answer's anybody's guess."

Armstrong looked dejected, and Fargo lowered his fork. "I told you when I started this, Armstrong," Fargo said. "It's a real iffy kind of deal. I can't promise you that the kid's not going to take off and head for California. Hell, maybe he already has. Even if he

23

doesn't, I can't promise you that he'll find Dawber, or get taken in by him, or lead me to your ring. If Dawber hasn't sold it off."

"He hasn't," Armstrong said with conviction.

Fargo wasn't nearly so convinced, but held his tongue. His face must have given him away, though, because Armstrong repeated, more emphatically, "He hasn't, Fargo. My people would know. I am as certain of this as I am of the fact that we're sitting here."

"All right, Armstrong," Fargo said, lifting his fork again. "I believe you."

Maybe he *did* know. Armstrong had sure changed a lot since the last time he and Fargo crossed trails.

Armstrong was rich and Armstrong lived in a fancy house and dressed like a gent. It was a far cry from the old days, when he used to wear bucks, not unlike those Fargo favored, and haunted the brothels and bars up and down the Mississippi. He was as quick to jump into a fistfight as he was a game of cards, too.

Those were the days.

Fargo swallowed his beef, then took a sip of wine. That was pretty fancy, too, an excellent vintage.

"What the hell happened to you, Armstrong?" Fargo blurted out, sweeping a hand toward the expensive paintings, the elegant furnishings. "Jesus Christ, here I expected to find you bar-crawling, but you've got all this? How on earth?"

Surprisingly, Armstrong flushed to the color of a tomato, and Fargo thought again. Hurriedly he added, "Didn't mean to be so nosy. Sorry if I asked the wrong question."

But Armstrong shook his head. "No, you have a right to know, Fargo." And then he shrugged. "I just fell into it, that's all."

"Just fell into it?" Fargo laughed. "Armstrong, I got to find somebody to kick your butt for not hollering for help on the way down."

Armstrong laughed, too, and something in him which had been stiff and cold relaxed, softened. "Hell. You were long gone when I got into that game."

"Game?"

"Fargo, I tell you true. Everything I am, everything you see in this house, I owe to one lousy game of seven card stud poker."

Fargo leaned back in his chair and cocked a brow. "Don't mean to cast aspersions, but back when I knew you, most of your poker games were lucky to come up with a five dollar pot."

"Yeah," agreed Armstrong. "Well, one night one of those penny-ante players came up short and wanted to stay in. He took this red ring off his finger and tossed it in. And I'll be damned if I wasn't holding a full house, aces over queens."

Something in Fargo's head clicked. He said, "Red ring? You don't mean to tell me that—"

"Yup," said Armstrong. "One and the same as I'm currently missing. Hell, I didn't know it was a ruby until years later. I figure the fellow that lost it to me didn't know it either, or he wouldn't have been so carefree with it."

Armstrong paused to take a sip of wine, then he shrugged. "I just thought it was my lucky ring, because right after that game, my luck turned. I mean, it really turned, Fargo. For a while there, it seemed like I couldn't sink a pick into the ground without hitting gold, couldn't buy a riding hack without it turning out to be a grand racehorse, couldn't set a line of traps without them coming up solid mink."

Fargo just shook his head.

Even if that ring had turned out to be brass and glass, its loss had to be hard on Armstrong, who'd always been one for signs and omens and charms. He'd always been on the watch for owls by daylight or the moon turning reddish or signs in the grasses and trees and such.

Fargo used to think it was just one of his idiosyncracies, but it looked like one of them had finally paid off for him.

"So you can see why I must have it back, Fargo," Armstrong continued, and his tone changed abruptly.

He was almost pleading, now, and his voice had lowered to a whisper.

"I tell you, Fargo, I'm afraid to go out of the house. Hell, I'm afraid to receive visitors. You're the only man—other than the police—that I've seen since it happened. Since that little monster picked it right off my goddamn hand!"

Fargo didn't know what to say. He'd never seen Armstrong in such a state, and he was almost embarrassed by it.

Clearly, he had to find that damned ring.

And Toby had best be doing what he was supposed to do.

5

Toby was down by the river, one hand in his pocket, gripping his money, the other rolling a wooden slug back and forth over his fingers. He'd only ever had anyone chase him for stealing a horse on three occasions.

Of course, he'd only tried to thieve four horses. But at least the men who chased him didn't have a loud whistle to blow, and Toby had outrun all of them.

Even without the horses.

He guessed that some things about being young worked in his favor. For instance, he didn't have an old beer belly, and he didn't get out of breath before he'd run fifty yards.

Of course, he hadn't grown any whiskers yet, save for three hairs on his left cheek that just turned out to be pesky. His voice still cracked every once in a while, too.

Most days, he just wanted to be older in the worst way. Today, though, he wished he was younger. That kid, the one that had run him over, had only been about twelve or so.

But then, maybe he wasn't one of Dawber's boys.

Criminy, he didn't know, and frankly, he gave up. He'd try again tomorrow. As it was, he'd stayed on the streets till long after dark, trying to pick one out of the mob, but had no luck. Right now, the river and the streets and the sky above were pretty much the same shade of black.

He turned back toward the street that rān along the dock. There were a few lights on, he guessed.

Bars, most likely, by the laughter and raucous sounds that emerged from them.

He stuck his head-scratching hand into his pocket and started away from the stench of the river and up toward the street. Mayhap somebody would finally sell him a drink around here.

He'd never had a drink except when he was back at the orphanage and his friend Bass had swiped the janitor's bottle of rotgut. That had been pretty awful, but then, he'd been a child of eleven at the time, and Bass's purloined Who Hit John had been cheap. He'd admire to try a real drink now.

Now that he was practically all grown up, that was. He had a real job and everything!

And besides, he didn't figure that this Dawber worked his kids at night. The streets, jammed and sunny during the day, had pretty much faded, their crowds dispersing with the sun's light. There were just a few drunks—and a few questionable looking men—hanging around now under the feeble light from the gas lamps. He'd do better to start hanging around in the morning.

He was almost to the Little Cougar Café and headed toward the Green Parrot, a bar beyond it that seemed to be doing considerable business. They had a wide front window painted with pictures of big, colorful birds, too, the kind he supposed you'd only see if you went somewhere that had a zoo. He liked that.

He was just passing the mouth of an alley—giving it a wide berth, too—when a voice said, "Wouldn't try the Green Parrot if I was you."

Since the voice didn't sound threatening, he stopped and turned toward it. All he saw were deep shadows.

"Who's there?" he asked. "And what's wrong with the Green Parrot?"

A boy stepped out of the shadows. He was ragtag, blond-headed, appeared to be about three or four years younger than Toby, and he was smiling. So, of course, Toby was suspicious right off. He hadn't been on his own for all these years without learning something about smiles, and how they lied.

He pulled his hands from his pockets and relaxed them, but they were ready to be balled into fists at the first sign of any funny business on the part of the strange boy.

But the kid just kept grinning at him. "They'd throw you outta the Parrot, quick as that," he said with a snap of his fingers. "Probably throw you in the river, to boot. You all right?"

Toby wrinkled his brow. "What?" he said.

"I asked, was you all right," said the boy. Suddenly, he stuck out his hand and Toby jumped back. But it wasn't aimed at him like a weapon. It was extended. The boy said, "Hell, I ain't gonna try to slug you. I already ran you over once today!"

Toby relaxed a little and shook hands, saying, "That was you? This afternoon?"

"Yup," the boy said cockily. "I got away from that whistle-blowin' bastard, too, thanks to you bein' in the road. I'm Toledo, by the way."

"Howdy, Toledo," Toby said, and introduced himself.

"Glad to meet you, Toby," Toledo replied. "You got a place to stay?"

Just in case this kid turned out to be on the level, so to speak, Toby lied and shook his head no.

Toledo nodded. "Been watchin' you. Didn't figure you'd hang out down at the docks this late if you had anyplace else to be. Christ, they stink!" He made a face, then leaned closer, confiding, "It's the fish guts, y'know."

It was Toby's turn to nod. He arched a brow and asked, "So, why you been watchin' me? A thing like that could get a feller mad."

Toledo brought his hands up, palms out. "Don't get me wrong, there, Toby. You out of a job? You got no folks?"

"Right on both counts, if it's any of your goddamn business."

Amazingly, Toledo laughed. "Don't suppose you're opposed to a little nefarious behavior, are you? Sub rosa, so to speak?"

"Huh?"

Toledo gave a little snort and then said, "I mean, you opposed to pickin' a pocket or two? A little distract and swipe in the stores? A little of the handbag grab and run?"

Toby straightened a little. It looked like he'd hit the jackpot. And on the first night, too!

He said, "Got no moral opposition to it. Other than the fact that I'd get caught and end up in jail or the workhouse."

"How old are you?" Toledo asked.

"What's it to you?"

Toledo shrugged. "Just askin', that's all. You're what? Fourteen? Fifteen?"

Toby stepped a big mental foot on the part of him that wanted to claim his true age, which would be all of sixteen next week, and said, "Fifteen," just as proud as he could.

"Figured as much," said Toledo. He stepped forward and slung his arm around Toby's shoulders, a feat he managed despite being the shorter of the two by a good six inches.

"Now, you come along with me, Toby," he said, even as Toby wiggled out from under his arm. Toledo sighed, and said, "You're gonna have to learn to trust some folks, there, Toby, if'n you want to run with my gang."

"Your gang?" Toby said with a snort.

"My gang. You know, my bunch."

Toby wanted nothing to do with a bunch of street toughs unless they were working for a man named Dawber. But then, maybe he should stay in good with this kid, if he could.

You never could tell what would happen. What if Dawber couldn't be turned up, or wasn't in St. Louis anymore? What if Fargo then dumped him and rode off and never paid him another cent?

Toby figured it would be worth the effort to stay friends with the blond boy.

"Well, not *my* gang, really," Toledo waffled, and Toby took heart.

"Whose gang, then?" he asked.

"A friend of mine," came Toledo's cryptic answer. "I already mentioned you to him. He wants to meet up with you."

Toby cocked a brow. "How do I know you're on the up and up with me? I mean, this friend of yours could knock me over the head and leave me for dead in the river. Not that he'd get nothin' for his labor but a lousy two bits," he lied. Then, just to push home the point, he added, "If that."

"Hey, Toby," Toledo urged, "take a chance. Just come and meet him. He can teach you everything you need to know. I know you got good hands. I seen you rollin' that coin over your fingers."

Toby was surprised by this. If he'd known anybody was watching, he would have done something fancy. He said, "It's a wood advertisin' slug, not a coin."

"Whatever, it was fine," replied Toledo, and placed his arm around Toby's shoulders again. "Come on," he said, giving Toby a little tug. I bet you ain't had a good feed in a long time, huh?"

Toby said, "I am kinda hungry, I guess." Actually, his stomach *was* growling some. Funny how you could have a great big lunch like he'd had, then bread and cheese on the docks, and still be starving a few hours later. It didn't seem fair, somehow.

"Right," he said.

"Well, let's go meet the man and get us some supper, then!"

Shrugging, Toby gave in to gravity. He marched down the street at Toledo's side.

He comforted himself that if Toledo wanted him to meet the wrong "man," at least he'd get a free dinner out of it.

They walked down the street, turned down an alley,

then crossed over the next street, and wove between buildings until Toby, who had been trying to keep track of where they were going, was completely lost.

It only struck him after the fact that this was what Toledo was purposefully trying to do, to confuse him. He found it a little annoying, but at least Toledo took him past the same corner twice.

He'd remember that.

At long last, they came to a tall building, still within the sound of the slowly rushing river. They turned into the side street, entered it beneath a large NO TRESPASSING sign, and climbed three stories' worth of rickety wooden stairs to a narrow, windowless corridor.

Squinting to see by the taper that Toledo had produced and lit, Toby followed. The corridor ended in a rough wooden door, at which Toby rapped softly in a pattern of sorts: twice, pause, three times, pause, then once more.

Frankly, the place they were in had the hair on Toby's neck standing up. The first floor had been all right, he supposed, even though the building looked long deserted. But with each narrow set of stairs that they climbed, the cobwebs above became more numerous and threatening, somehow. The scratches and peeps of scurrying rats, somewhere out of sight, became thicker and louder, and his situation seemed more ominous.

By the time anyone ever came to that door, he was fairly certain that Toledo was bringing him up here to bash his head in, go through his pockets, then toss him off the roof.

Or feed him to those unseen rats.

Already tense as a jackrabbit who thought he heard a coyote, he balled his hands into fists, intending to give as good as he got.

After all, he told himself, Toledo was younger, wasn't he? And smaller? He'd have to be a mighty tricky fighter to down Toby Jones!

He wouldn't have to be awful tricky to do me some damage, though, Toby thought, and behind Toledo's back, raised his fists.

But just then, the door creaked open an inch, letting a thin wedge of light out into the hall.

"Who goes there?" whispered a scratchy voice with a curious accent.

"Toledo," said the other boy.

"And what do you bring me?" whispered the voice in reply.

"A pretty treat," Toledo said smugly, and Toby took a step backward without realizing it. This was all just a little too spooky for him.

The door creaked open a little wider, and then a face appeared. "Well, now," the whisperer said, eyeing Toby. The owner of the voice was an older man, probably about fifty, Toby thought. He had a big, hooked nose, and his face was hatchet-narrow and topped by thinning gray hair that hung down in unkempt wisps.

Toby swallowed. If this was the fellow that he was supposed to find, all of a sudden Fargo's two hundred and fifty didn't seem like much. This man looked like an illustration out of a book, a book meant to scare little kids on All Hallow's Eve.

It was working, too.

An arm, clad in black and ending in a clawlike, skeletal hand, suddenly swung the door wide.

"Come in," said the skeleton man. He smiled, but Toby could tell there wasn't any humor behind it.

Toledo walked on in, and the man clucked his tongue at Toby, who was still frozen in place. "Come in, pretty," the man urged, still smiling. "Could I interest you in some beef stew?"

It occurred to Toby that indeed, there was a strong smell of stew—and pretty good beef and vegetable stew, at that—issuing through the door, tantalizing him. He licked his lips.

"Okay, Mister," he said, and took off his hat. "Smells good."

"That's my boy," Toby heard the man say as he brushed past and into a strange sort of wonderland. "That's my boy."

6

Fargo checked his pocket watch once he was outside of Armstrong's house. Nine o'clock. Still early. At least, for a certain kind of person.

The building looming behind him began to dim its lights, as was the case in the houses up and down the street. Well, he hoped they all slept well.

However, there was no rest for the wicked, and Fargo was surely in the sort of mood for a little wickedness.

Preferably, of the female variety.

He started walking down the street. If he was lucky, he could catch a passing cab at the cross street, then take a ride down to the docks. He'd drop in at the Riverside Hotel—surreptitiously, of course—and make sure Toby had checked in. And then he might see what kind of wildlife inhabited the local saloons.

Female wildlife, to be exact. His interlude with the charming Lola earlier in the day had left him hungry for more of the same.

He flagged down a cab at the corner, and was damned lucky to do it. The street traffic had thinned out considerably since he'd arrived at Armstrong's house for dinner.

It struck him that the high-toned part of St. Louis was dull, dull, dull.

Course, this was a Thursday night. Maybe on Fridays or Saturdays they threw caution to the wind and stayed up till ten.

As the horse clipped along, going ever closer to the seamy side of the city, there was a gradual change in the light level. And by the time he stepped down in front of the Red Door Saloon and handed a few coins up to the driver, the street lamps were fewer and farther between but the lamp light positively beamed from the windows.

He had a beer at the Red Door and shook a few hands. He said he was Drinkwater, Larry Drinkwater, just in from Des Moines, and by Holy God, that was some big river they had down here!

After that, he made his way down the street, stopping for another beer at the Dancing Lady—which had no ladies, dancing or otherwise, available while he was there—and then Murphy's Bar, and then the Gateway.

After he stopped for a long and satisfying piss in an alleyway, he walked another block and a half to the Riverside Hotel, and while the clerk was distracted by a nonexistent fight in the alley (which Fargo reported), he stole a look at the register. Toby Jones was there, all right, his name written in the big, loopy letters of a schoolboy.

Fargo slipped out before the clerk—who was bound to be unhappy with him—came back in, and hiked another block to the Little Cougar Café.

"Beer," he called to the barkeep over the crowd's hum. It was a nice place, he supposed. That is, if you were a river pirate or a cutthroat.

He carried his beer back to a corner table and began to look over the female contingent. All in all they were a sad lot, badly painted and badly aging and, he supposed, badly used. He sensed a thousand sad stories that he didn't want to hear.

Still, he sat back and let himself relax a little, trying to take it all in. As he sipped his warm beer, he wondered what Toby was up to.

* * *

"C'mon, c'mon," Toledo said, gesturing and grinning.

Toby walked slowly after him, all the while casting his gaze about, his eyes adjusting to the light. And what wondrous sights he saw!

The place was open and wide, an attic really, with boards haphazardly nailed down over the beams of the ceiling below. There were no windows, but a cheery fire in a crude hearth was lit at one end and a cook fire was ablaze at the other.

In the corner, a boy, wearing a long man's coat covered in tiny bells, stood on a box and pretended to stroke his nonexistent beard while two other boys tried to get into his pockets without his notice—or without jarring one of the bells.

They weren't having much luck, and the skeleton man left Toby to go to their assistance.

In another corner—the one Toledo was calling him toward—rich-smelling stew was being dished up by a tall, scraggly, redheaded kid.

On the way, he passed a group of three boys, two of whom were listening intently to the third, who was quizzing them on the correct way to fleece a shopkeeper without getting caught. Then he passed another quartet, one of whom was smoking a corncob pipe, and one of whom was entertaining the other three like a medicine show barker.

There were old trunks piled on trunks against the murky side walls, along with crates and boxes that seemed to be used for nightstands as well as makeshift walls for a sort of room. Sleeping pallets, ready for use or rolled up tight as blood-swollen ticks, were lined up along the wall.

Toledo and Toby, his head craning and twisting like an owl's, joined the short line at the stewpot and were each handed a full bowl and a spoon, then a hunk of bread. "You're new, eh?" asked the redheaded boy in charge of the stewpot.

Trying not to spill his stew, Toby shrugged.

"Reckon I am," he said, and lowered his nose to take a whiff of his dinner. "Stew looks grand. Smells good, too."

The redhead suddenly smiled. "Thanks. None'a these louts notice one way or t'other. My name's Rance. Rance Ketchum."

"I'm Toby. Toby Jones." He was going to stick out his hand, but couldn't decide whether to offer the one with the stew or the one with the bread.

Rance laughed and said, "We'll shake later."

Toledo rolled his eyes and said, "Jesus, why's everybody bein' so consarned polite all of a sudden? C'mon, Toby. Let's sit down over here."

Cally was cleaned up, changed, and ready when Big Mike called for her. Or rather, when he appeared at her door and grumbled, "Well? What's keepin' you?"

"Nothin'," she said, and stepped outside, locking the door behind her.

"Glad you didn't wear that stupid hat," he said as they started briskly up the street, circumnavigating the occasional drunk passed out in their path. "I like that one you got on now a lot better."

"Course you do, you lummox," she said, staring ahead. "You gave it to me."

"Knew there was a reason," he admitted grumpily. "I like red."

"Never let it be said that you don't have impeccable taste."

Mike grabbed her by the shoulder and none too gently hauled her about.

"Ouch!" she yelped, and batted at his hand.

"Don't get all highfalutin with me, sister," he warned.

"Not gettin' highfalutin," she said, rubbing her shoulder now that his big paw was gone. "It was an observation, dammit. I was agreeing with you!"

He shook his fist in her face. It was a move that was not wholly unexpected and not a bit unusual, and she stood her ground. "Someday, Cally . . ."

Innocently, she batted her eyelashes. "Yes, Michael?"

He cocked his head. "Aw, you're a pretty little thing, ain't you?" he said, his expression suddenly softening.

Then, just as quickly, it toughened up again, as if he were afraid someone might see his bedroom face out here in the street.

Silly man.

He said, "Just quit with them nickel words, all right? Save 'em for Dawber."

"Yes, Mike."

She wove her arm through his. Arm in arm, the oddly contented pair continued up the darkened street in silence.

Toby was nearly through his second bowl of stew—and practically certain he was in the right place—when the skeleton man came up and sat down on the crate across from him.

Old crates and trunks and boxes seemed to be the sole pieces of furniture in the place, except for one wooden rocking chair that no one was sitting in. Toby figured it was reserved for the man across from him.

"Did the food please you?" the man asked, and suddenly, it dawned on Toby what kind of accent the man had.

English. Kind of a mangled English accent, like maybe he was from an odd part of England, or maybe because it was softened by years in America. But it was English nonetheless.

"Yes, sir," Toby responded. "Mighty good. Thank you very much."

If his hat hadn't already been off, he would have doffed it.

"Good, good. Well, Toledo? Tell me about our friend, here."

"He's on the up and up, Dawber," Toledo said right out, and something in Toby gave a silent cheer. It was Dawber, then, and he was in the right place. For once, he had fallen into it. Maybe Fargo had brought him a side of luck along with that steak lunch.

"Just hangin' round the docks, like I told you he'd be. I watched him all afternoon, once I lost that flat-footed cop. Was he what you were lookin' for?"

Much to Toby's surprise, Dawber stuck out a bony hand and cuffed Toledo's ear. Toby jumped back a few inches, but then Toledo smiled. So did Dawber.

He turned toward Toby again. "Lad," he said, "if Toledo vouches for you, that's good enough for me. Welcome, my darling, to our little club."

"Thank you, sir," said Toby. He wondered if he should ask the man's name, although he already knew it. He wondered if he should try to act a little tougher, but then decided that he'd already been polite too long to change without appearing odd.

And he also wished that the man would knock off that "darling" and "my dear" and "my pretty" stuff. And what was the "looking for" business? Why would Dawber have been looking for him? He'd never been in St. Louis, not ever.

It was all pretty strange, but Toby said nothing.

Dawber leaned forward and put a hand on Toby's knee. "So, tell me boy," he said, his voice low and sincere and indicating all the parental concern in the world. "How long have you been on your own?"

Toby thought, *Oh, you're good,* but said, "Always, I reckon. Well, since I ran away from the orphanage." He'd made that part up while he was riding into town. He thought it might make him seem younger.

Dawber's eyes were full of sympathy. They were also, Toby realized, more than a little hypnotic. "A sad life, my boy, a very sad life," Dawber intoned. "And I suppose it's been here and there, catch as catch can in the interim?"

Toby twisted his face and said, "Huh?"

Dawber laughed, gave Toby's knee a last pat, and stood up. "Well, no more rooting through garbage cans for you, my lovely. You're working for Dawber now, and we live high!" He swept his arms wide to take in the whole attic, as if it were a magnificent palace.

Toby smiled, and Toledo gave Toby a none-too-gentle punch in the arm.

"You're with Dawber now, pal!" he crowed.

"Tomorrow is soon enough to begin, my boy," Dawber said with a cryptic smile and a wink, then walked away, across the attic, and disappeared behind a wall of crates. His "room," Toby supposed, for he saw lantern light bloom above the divider of old trunks.

Toledo stood up. "Empty bowls over there," he said, indicating a large box over by the cooking area. Dirty dishes were piled high on its top. "Then," Toledo continued, "I'll introduce you around to a few of the fellers."

"Fine with me," Toby replied. He hoped they'd give him a pallet to sleep on. He also hoped that it wouldn't have any bugs, like the thin mattress back at the Riverside Hotel.

It didn't occur to him until he'd dropped off his dirty bowl to ask how Toledo had managed to watch him all afternoon, report in to Dawber, then come back and spy on him some more, all without him knowing it.

Toledo just winked at him. "Tricks of the trade, Toby," he said. "Tricks of the trade! C'mon, I want you to meet Nimble Jack!"

7

Behind the walls of crates and boxes that formed barriers between it and the outer room that housed the boys, sat Dawber's bed. And on Dawber's bed sat Dawber himself, arms stretched wide over the headboard, looking like the King of Sheba.

If indeed Sheba had a king to go with its fabled queen, Cally thought.

She and Big Mike had just settled down on a couple of crates, which formed the only other furniture in the attic, inside Dawber's "room" or out.

Dawber said, "Go on, Michael, my lad, pour the drinks. You know where the bottle is."

Mike didn't hesitate. As usual. And Cally rolled her eyes, although she made sure nobody saw her do it. You didn't want to tick off Dawber. And you especially didn't want to irritate Big Mike in front of Dawber. He always had to make a big show out of everything when he was with his idol.

And idol was exactly what Cally had come to believe Dawber was to Big Mike. That such a scrawny, woebegone, ugly little man could command such respect from Big Mike was almost laughable.

Well, you could laugh, but Mike would knock you six ways from seven for your transgression.

Having already been knocked about more times than she could count, Cally wasn't much in the mood to push things.

Mike handed her the drink after he handed Dawber his—naturally—and sat back down on his crate. They all took a sip in silence, and then Mike asked, "Anything new, Dawber?"

And Cally was thinking that she really had no need to come to these little meetings. They were always the same. Drink, any new topics, some plans about the boys, more drinks, she wondered off to see about the boys, and then they left.

Ho hum.

"Got a new lad today," Dawber said, gazing through the liquid in his upheld glass. "Looks to be a fine lad. Very pretty. A bit on the old side—sixteen if he's a day—but very pretty. I believe, my dear, that he just may be the one I've been looking for."

"Yeah, Dawber?" Mike said, like a schoolboy at the feet of his master. It was embarrassing. "What's he in for? Pickpocketin'? The old cash drop? Swipe and run? Or maybe . . ."

Dawber shook his head. "Possibly, possibly. But that, my dear, remains to be seen. We shall begin in earnest on the morrow."

Cally saw her chance. "Where is this child, Dawber?" she asked after she'd drained her glass. Dawber was big on everyone drinking all they were given. "I'd like to meet him."

"Certainly you're excused, my dear," Dawber purred, although she noticed that his eyes flicked to her empty glass with some satisfaction. "You may tour the camp, so to speak." He raised a hand and flicked his fingers at her, motioning her away.

She was dismissed, and she took advantage of it by rising quickly and exiting through the break in the wall of crates. The bastard. Both of them were bastards, really, each in his own way. As much experience as she'd had—and she'd had thousands of times more than most women, she thought—she'd never understand men, not really.

Oh, you could understand and anticipate them the

same way you could anticipate a five-year-old child. But yet, they continued to surprise you.

She rounded the crate wall and entered the attic proper. Most of the boys had settled in for the night, but a few were gathered down at the far end, probably listening to one of Baltimore Bill's tall tales again, and another, smaller group was hunkered down close to where the roof sloped to meet the floor.

She overheard enough to know that they were shooting dice.

At last, her gaze lit upon a new face. He was indeed pretty. If he were cleaned up, she thought, he might even have looked angelic, like in one of those Italian paintings. He was talking with Toledo and Nimble Jack in very low and serious tones, but she decided to butt in anyway.

"You must be the new lad," said a distinctly feminine voice, and Toby's head came up with a jerk. A woman? Here?

But what a woman! Despite his youth, he took her in up, down, and sideways with a quick sweep of his eyes, and she was a knockout, all right. Sweeping off his hat, he rose to his feet, barely noticing that the other boys, the fair Toledo and the dark-haired Nimble Jack, had done the same.

"Yes, ma'am, I am," he said, and by the grace of God managed to neither stutter nor let his voice break.

"And your name?

Toby told her, and she said, "I'm Calista Teach, but you can call me Cally for short, Toby. Everybody does."

"Yes ma'am," he said.

She shook her head and smiled. "And you can drop that 'ma'am.' I'm just Cally."

"Everybody on the streets knows Cally," Nimble Jack said proudly, his dark, shaggy hair falling in his eyes as he nodded.

Toby didn't exactly think that being known by everybody on the streets was such a good thing for a pretty lady like Cally, but Nimble Jack seemed to believe it was pretty grand. So did Toledo, who nodded enthusiastically.

"How's that cough of Tinker's coming along?" she asked Toledo, then looked around, searching the attic. "I don't see him."

"Oh, he's doin' real good," said Toledo. "You want I should wake him up for you?"

"No, no," Cally said. "Don't wake him. Don't wake anybody. You children work too hard all day to be disturbed in your slumbers. How's that cut on Wally's leg?"

"It pussed somethin' awful for a day after you put that salve on it, Cally," offered Nimble Jack. "But it's nigh on healed over. And Wally don't limp no more, either."

"Glad to hear it."

Cally turned toward Toby again, who had been watching her as if she were the only thing in the world. "So, tell me about yourself, Toby? Where'd you come from, and how did you fall in with this den of thieves?"

Toby swallowed hard and croaked, "Ma'am?"

She laughed. It was like music, it was so pretty, and then she said, "I'm just teasing you, Toby."

"No, she ain't," offered Toledo happily. "We're thieves, all right, and I guess you could call this place a den of 'em."

A grinning Cally flicked her fingers at him. "Go on with you, Toledo Corcoran. I want to talk to Mr. Toby Jones."

Toledo and Nimble Jack stood up, although somewhat reluctantly, and ambled over to the corner.

"So tell me, sweetie," Cally began. "What's life been like for you?"

Later that evening, a disappointed Fargo left the Little Cougar Café. In each place he'd stopped before

44

ending at the Little Cougar, the beer had been warm and watered, the women had been ugly and far too friendly even for his taste, and the company—any company he'd want to keep, that was—had been nonexistent.

He'd stayed at the Little Cougar as long as he had because they didn't water the beer. As much as the other places, anyhow. And also because he had one of those odd feelings that he was, well, supposed to be there.

But by eleven, he gave up and decided to go back to his hotel. It was a good walk away, but he figured that he needed the air after all that beer. And also, after his fruitless search for a woman.

Oh, he could have had his pick of them. But as close to desperate as he was, he figured to be above the grossly fat, the toothless, the aged, and the obviously diseased. And it seemed to him those were the only gals "on duty" on the riverfront this evening.

Dammit.

Dawber leaned out his "door" and cast a quick eye over the boys. His darlings. His little moneymaking darlings. What could be sweeter?

"Time to be turning in, Charlie," he whispered to two boys, still sitting up, talking. "You, too, Herman, my love."

"Right," Charlie whispered back, and the two boys slipped down onto their pallets.

Dawber walked out, then around the big room. Blowing out lamps and candles as he went, silently checking on this boy or that. He had a dozen and a half at the moment, counting this new recruit.

He paused at the foot of Toby's bedroll, watching the boy's angelic face in sleep. Lovely, just lovely. He'd fit in anywhere, this Toby. Much too nice to use on the docks, but it was just as well. He had far grander plans for this one.

Dawber scratched his balding head. Too bad he wasn't back in England anymore. He'd had connections, by God. He could have got this boy to where the takings were better than good!

But he wasn't in England anymore, he reminded himself. Hadn't been for almost thirty years. He'd been stuck here in these beastly colonies for almost half his life.

What a shame. And he'd been such a blithering idiot, trying to hoodwink Edwin Partridge! How was he to know that Partridge would have him hauled into the Old Bailey, and how could he possibly have known that the judge would be Partridge's second cousin?

He supposed he should feel lucky that they hadn't hanged him, even though being banished from the realm for life was a close second.

But he'd adapted. He had his boys. He'd been run out of New York City, and run out of Chicago, and he'd likely be run out of St. Louis one day. But while he remained?

It was a living.

All the lamps and candles taken care of, Dawber moved toward the one spot of brightness in the entire attic, which was the fan of light that emerged from his doorway. He entered, pulled the shabby curtain to give himself some privacy from prying little eyes. And carefully, soundlessly, pried up a floorboard.

From the cavity beneath, he pulled a small strongbox, which he opened with a key he wore around his neck, concealed under his clothing.

He dropped the key back into hiding before he opened the lid. He took great relish in this, always, and never failed to act surprised and giddy at what he found there.

This time was no different.

When the first glints caught his eye, he had to cover his mouth to keep from giggling. And when the box was open all the way? Let joy be unconfined!

Gold coins, scattered as if in a pirate's treasure chest—for that was exactly what it was, only in miniature—mingled with purloined jewelry. It was the best of the best—well, part of it—of what the boys had brought in for over twenty-five years, and from around the globe. He had other hidey-holes, concealed about the room.

But this was his favorite cache of goodies. Three strings of fabulous pearls, a diamond brooch, two sets of lovely diamond earrings, and a very large—and very famous—diamond necklace formed the glittering and warm backdrop for emerald and sapphire trinkets and baubles, deep red rubies, and glittering golden coins and shining jewelry.

He sifted his fingers through it, felt its weight, reveled in its beauty. He held up a diamond earring and studied the twinkle in the light from his candle, admiring it as another man might admire his firstborn son.

He loved the way the gold warmed to his touch, and he loved the manner in which the gems clung to their coolness. He loved the fire of his rubies, and deep ocean blue of his sapphires, and the rich kelly green of his emeralds.

And oh, the jangle of his golden coins! Now there was music. A symphony!

"Mr. Dawber? Sir?"

Quickly, he threw a protective arm around his hoard and looked toward the door, ready to lay a cane over whoever had disturbed him. His boys knew better!

But it was Toby, the new boy, with one fist rubbing a sleepy eye. "Mr. Dawber, I'm sorry to bother you, but where's the . . . you know?" he asked groggily.

"Downstairs," Dawber said a little crankily.

"Where downstairs?" the lad asked.

Suddenly, Dawber felt a little bad. Which was highly unusual for him. "Take a candle, boy, and go down one flight. You can piss out the window or shit in the corner. Or lean out the window, if you think you can keep your balance. God knows the others do."

Young Toby's eyes opened a little wider at this suggestion, but he said, "Yes, sir," and wandered off.

A few moments later, Dawber heard the scratch of a candle, then the creak of the attic door being opened.

Dawber let himself relax, then shook his head. He was a fool, thinking everyone was after his loot. Why, nobody even knew it existed save for himself! Especially a skinny fifteen-year-old boy who had gotten up in the middle of the night—and in a strange place—and felt the need to empty his bladder.

"Let it go," he chided himself softly as he listened to young Toby Jones carefully thumping his way down the narrow stair. "Just let it go, my dear Dawber. You have other fish to fry."

8

Fargo walked down the deserted streets. Well, they were deserted at first glance, anyway. Drunks were passed out on the sidewalk here and there. Some of the gaslights were broken, emitting a soft hiss but no light, and he had to watch his step lest he trip over a prone figure.

Sounds came from the occasional alley, the soft groans and grunts of hurried lovers. Or rather, clients with prostitutes.

This was the industrial district, or had been at one time. Most of the buildings he passed were falling down factories. Some of them were posted with NO TRESPASSING signs, which, judging by the busted-out, glassless windows and the crossbars ripped from the doors, had been largely ignored.

Some had been left open to the wind and whoever was brave enough to take shelter there.

And a few seemed to be taking care of business as usual. Smoke poured from their chimneys, lamps glowed in the upper floor windows, and he could hear hammering and the faint hum of foot-pedaled machinery, the creak of chains fighting with pulleys.

But those last were few and far between. It was a dying part of the city, home to warrens of waifs and drunkards, prostitutes and criminals, and the lost of all persuasions.

Fargo mulled this over, growing thoughtful and perhaps careless because of the emptiness of the street and—to be honest—all the beer he'd imbibed. His head was down, keeping an eye on the drunk sprawled ahead on the corner.

And just as he circumnavigated the warm body on the sidewalk, he ran straight into something. He would have said it was a brick wall, except for the fact that it was wearing a tartan vest. Fargo's nose hit it at the top button.

"Hey!" shouted a man as Fargo stumbled backward, regained his balance, and looked upward.

The man was a giant, six-feet-seven at least, and heavily built. And he looked none too happy.

Even in his current state of muzziness, Fargo's first inclination was to ball up his fists and gather himself, but he had the presence of mind to remember who he was supposed to be. And Larry Drinkwater from Des Moines wouldn't launch into this hulk.

So he said, "Sorry, pal, right sorry."

"You oughta watch where the hell you're walkin'," grumbled the behemoth.

Only then did Fargo notice that the giant wasn't alone. A woman stood beside him, a woman who, he automatically knew, deserved better things than this street, this city, and the tattered but tidy clothes she was wearing.

And especially the giant oaf she was with.

Fargo doffed his hat and gave a semblance of a bow. "Excuse me, miss."

"That's more like it," muttered the big man, then added, with more volume, "You take my advice, Mister, you'll go camp out in an alley for the night. Unless you got some money."

Fargo knew a sly but probing question when he heard one, and said, "No, no money." He shook his head sadly. "Spent it on that last beer."

The woman seemed to be studying him, albeit in a different way than the man. She seemed curious, and her gaze was gentle. Unlike the man, who was still sizing him up.

She said, "Why don't we take him with us, Mike?

He won't last five minutes out here on his own. Why, just look at him!"

Fargo made a show of looking down at himself and pretending to be bemused, but he caught a glimpse of Mike's frown. It was an ugly thing, too.

"Cally, you're about two steps away from the loony bin," Mike growled. "I'll show you what we ought to do with him."

And with that, Mike shot out one enormous fist and punched Fargo squarely in the chest. It knocked him back five feet, and he landed on his ass.

As he struggled to get some air back into his lungs, he heard Mike laugh like a braying donkey, and the woman, Cally, shouting, "You big, dumb brute! He was just standin' there!"

Fargo finally caught his breath, and struggled to his feet. The woozy feeling he'd had from the beer was long gone, replaced by adrenaline. But his judgement still wasn't exactly the best, because he put his head down and charged Mike, full tilt.

He butted the son of a bitch right in the belly, and he must have taken him completely by surprise, because this time it was Mike who flew backward and landed on his backside.

You're in for it now, Fargo thought belatedly. The man was nearly twice his size.

Cally's eyes grew wide and she clasped her hands over her mouth. But the big man did something completely unanticipated.

He laughed.

In fact, he fairly roared with laughter.

Fargo cocked his head to one side and blinked.

Mike pulled himself up to his feet and, between chuckles, said, "By Christ, you got a load of sand for such a skinny little pip-squeak."

He stuck out his hand, and Fargo took it. "Mike's my name," the man said. "Big Mike Matthews. You got a moniker?"

"Larry," Fargo said. "Larry Drinkwater. From Des Moines."

"Pleased to meetcha, Larry Drinkwater from Des Moines," Big Mike roared happily. "This here's Cally Teach."

"It's Calista, actually," Cally said in a small voice.

"Cally," said Big Mike, correcting her. And with that utterance, Fargo knew that their relationship, if they had a personal one (and it looked like they did), was doomed.

He'd help to doom it, if it needed a little push.

Big Mike threw an arm around his shoulders. "C'mon, Drinkwater, ol' buddy. Let's go an' get us a beer. How's Des Moines, these days? Ain't been there since it was nothing but a cluster'a huts an' a fort."

Another beer wasn't exactly what Fargo wanted—or needed—but he figured, why look a gift horse—or in this case, a gift contact—in the mouth? Besides, he wanted some more time to gaze at the fair Calista.

So the two of them set off, back down the way Fargo had come, with Cally trailing behind.

She was humming softly, Fargo noted.

Big Mike studied this Drinkwater character over the top of his beer mug. Seemed a right enough feller, but Mike still had his suspicions.

Drinkwater was sure dressed like he was from Des Moines, all right. Not that Big Mike was sure what they dressed like up there nowadays, but if there was a way, this was probably it.

He didn't talk too much or brag himself up—the latter of which was one of the things that had Mike a tad nervous. Also, he seemed just a little too damned keen on Cally.

Oh, it was nothing overt, mind you. He just kept on glancing at her out of the corner of his eye, and he looked like he admired what he saw. Now, that was fine if Drinkwater was going to turn out to be a paying customer, but Drinkwater didn't strike Big Mike as the type who'd have to pay for it. At least, not too often.

It rubbed Mike the wrong way, that look on Drinkwater's face. But he purely admired the way old Drinkwater had picked himself up and belly-butted him out in the street! That took sand, by God.

And it went far enough with Mike to overlook those reasons he had for distrusting Larry Drinkwater, late of Des Moines.

For now, anyway.

He drained his beer and slammed the mug back on the table. "So, Drinkwater," he said, "what brings you to our fair city?"

The boys at the next table thought that was pretty funny, and started laughing. Big Mike half rose from his chair and shot them an evil look, and they quieted right down. One even said, "Uh, sorry . . ."

That was more like it.

Drinkwater observed this, and looked at Mike with a raised brow. "You're some sort of big shot around this neck of the woods, are you?"

"That I am," Mike replied with more than a little sense of pride.

"If you mean, is everybody and their brother afraid of him, the answer is yes," added Cally. She was in the third chair at the table, leaning back against the corner, and looking tired.

No, more used up than tired. For the millionth time, Mike had second thoughts about using Cally in this way as his bitch, his whore, his support . . . then did what he usually did when struck with a moral question. He ordered another beer.

"Don't believe you answered my question, Drinkwater," he said.

"Me?" Fargo replied. "Not much of a story there. I'm from Des Moines, but then, I already told you that. Spent some time up in St. Paul, but the Lutherans got to me."

He laughed, but when everyone else at the table stayed silent, he added, "It was pretty damned dull up there."

"What'd you do up in St. Paul, Mr. Drinkwater?" asked Cally.

"Little of this, a little of that," Drinkwater said cryptically. Then he lowered his head and leaned forward. "Mostly, the old badger game, if you gotta know. Like that. Lost my partner to a goddamn Lutheran dirt farmer, and now I'm at loose ends."

Big Mike burst out laughing. "I knew there was something I liked about you, Drinkwater!" He slapped the man on his Des Moines-suited back and nearly knocked him from his chair.

Which only made him laugh all the harder.

Fargo didn't like it.

He didn't like it one bit.

Here he was, trying to sleep on a lumpy sofa in Cally's front room while Big Mike was sleeping in the same bed with her, back down the hall.

It made him mad. Made him crazy, in fact. But there was nothing he could do about it. Not for the time being, anyway.

If he was going to hang around the docks for a few days or a few weeks—however long it took—he'd need to fit in. And what better way to accomplish that than to be one of Big Mike Matthews's friends?

At least, he thought he was. Just to be on the safe side, though, he'd waited until they retired, then he'd taken the last of his money and hidden it back behind some pots and pans.

He didn't think Big Mike would look on him so kindly if it was known that he'd been holding out almost seven hundred dollars on them.

At least they weren't making any noise back there. Now, that would have really been the kicker! But there was only the soft sound of Big Mike's snores, which had begun roughly five minutes after he and Cally had gone down the hall to the bedroom.

Fargo supposed he'd best be grateful for small favors.

He closed his eyes and tried to sleep, but found that all he could do was worry about Toby, wonder about Dawber, and fret about finding him. Maybe this Big

Mike knew him. Hell, he seemed to know everybody on the dockside.

Up in the high-toned part of town, Armstrong was sleeping in his bed while the big paddle wheels silently coursed up and down the Mississippi outside his window. Here, it stank of rotting fish and unbathed bodies and human waste and poverty.

And greed. Couldn't forget greed. Here at the docks, that simple five letter word was at the heart of the matter.

"Drinkwater?"

A whisper.

"Still awake," he whispered back. He couldn't see her, but he could smell her perfume. Lemon verbena, he thought. What the hell was she doing out here? And more to the point, what would Big Mike do if he woke and found her gone?

She emerged out of the gloom, wearing a long nightgown. White, he thought it was, although it could have been any light color.

"Are you all right?" she whispered.

"I am now," he replied with a grin.

She let that pass and said, "I just wanted to warn you. I come out at about five in the mornin' to fix a basket for a sick friend. I'll try to be quiet, but you might hear some rattling. Just roll over and ignore me, okay?"

Fargo, whose trousers suddenly felt much too tight, said, "I'll roll over, Miss Cally, but there's no way I could ignore you."

She smiled at him and then disappeared just as quickly as she had appeared. The scent of her perfume lingered for a moment, and then was gone, too.

"Damn!" Fargo hissed under his breath. This was going to be tougher than he'd imagined.

9

Toby rose abruptly to the sound of somebody banging a frying pan with a metal ladle and the sight of Dawber, standing in the middle of the room, shouting, "That's it, my pretties! Rise and shine! There's a new day ahead full of trinkets and goodies!"

Rubbing his eyes, Toby sat up, then unwound himself from his pallet and stood up. Today was going to be his day for learning. Learning what, he had no idea. But he was sort of looking forward to it.

On the other hand, he was still a little scared, and wished he could lay his hands on this little treasure stash of Dawber's. He'd take every ruby ring he found—that is, provided there was more than one— and hightail it faster than you could say succotash!

Maybe he'd do a little snooping, if he got the chance.

But it seemed that Dawber wasn't about to allow him one.

After breakfast, which consisted of bread and cheese and water and big, red apples all around, most of the other boys were sent out to the streets to scavenge what they could.

Toby and Toledo were held back, though.

Dawber made him stand in the middle of the room while he slowly walked around and around him, scratching his chin and making *hmmm* sounds. After the fifth such circle, Toby finally asked, "What? What you lookin' for, Mr. Dawber?"

"Just Dawber," he said, never taking his hand away from his chin. "And nothing in particular, my boy. Just looking."

Toby closed his eyes and sighed.

"There!" shouted Dawber, and when Toby looked up, Dawber's finger was pointed at him.

"There what?" Toby asked, startled.

But Dawber turned to Toledo and said, "You see it, boy? Just then?"

Toledo was all smiles. "Yessir, I did! He'll do fine."

"Once we hone a fine point on it . . ." Dawber added, trailing off.

Toby was aching to know just what it was that he'd done, and in what manner they were going to hone a point on it—or him—but kept his mouth shut. He figured they'd just ignore him, anyway.

"Clothes first," Dawber suddenly announced, stabbing a bony finger into the air. "Clothes make the man, right, Toledo?" he added as he scurried away, toward a trunk in the corner.

"What's he doin'?" Toby hissed to Toledo.

Brushing an unruly lock of blond hair out of his eyes, Toledo just grinned, then zippered a finger across his lips.

Toby rolled his eyes.

"Ah-ha!" cried Dawber from the corner. Toby looked, and saw him holding up a ridiculous suit of clothes, all dark blue velvet and what looked like—God forbid—ruffles. Dawber tossed it over his arm and continued with his rummaging.

In a few moments he produced a pair of shoes, then another pair, and started back toward Toby and Toledo. He thrust them forward.

"Try them on," he said, grinning in a self-satisfied way.

Toby took them, albeit reluctantly. "Why?" he asked.

The smile faded from Dawber's face. "Because I said so, laddie. From now on, you'll do everything I say. Understand?"

Well, that got Toby's back up, and he said, "Why should I?"

Before Toby could flinch away, Dawber's hand was firmly around his neck. He pulled Toby close, his foul breath wafting across Toby's face, and said, "Because I'm feeding you. Because I protect you. Because I take care of you. And because I'll kill you and toss your sorry carcass in the river if you ever cross me. No matter how fast and far you run, no matter how many times you change your name, I will find you, my pretty, and slice your lovely throat. Do you understand?"

Toby tried to gulp, but it got caught on Dawber's bony hand. So, his watering eyes bugging from the pressure, he nodded.

Dawber let go, and Toby collapsed on the wooden slats of the floor, coughing and choking and holding his neck. The son of a bitch was mighty strong for such a frail-looking old shit, and Toby believed every word he'd said. He'd seen Dawber's eyes close-up—closer than he ever wanted to again—and they meant business.

All of a sudden, he was wishing really hard that he'd never tried to steal Fargo's horse. That he'd been in Chicago at the time instead of outside St. Louis. That he'd been anywhere except where Fargo was.

But that now it was too late. He was in it, for certain sure.

"There's a good boy," Dawber said with a smile, as if the last five seconds hadn't even transpired.

"Now, put on the clothes," he went on. "They may not fit, but we'll have our darling Cally take care of that, won't we?" He tipped his head. "Toledo, off with you, now. You've dallied too long, and there are pockets to pick and purses to be had!"

"Right, Dawber!" Toledo answered gleefully, and started for the door.

Slowly, he throat still throbbing, Toby stood up and began changing into his new suit.

It took Fargo a few seconds to remember just where he'd woken up, and why. But it all came rushing back to him: the beer, Big Mike, the beer, Cally, and the beer. But mostly, Cally.

Well, he'd achieved his goal, anyway. Now he had a contact on the docks, and a seemingly important one, too, if Big Mike was to be believed. The nearness of Cally—with her nice smell and her beautiful face and figure—would be a distraction, but he imagined he could handle it.

He hoped.

He swung his legs over the side of the lumpy sofa and stood, stretching out the kinks.

A glance out the window told him it was around ten, judging by the sun. He'd slept too long. Too many beers did that to a man.

He called, "Cally? Mike?"

No answer.

But when he ambled out to the kitchen, he found a note, weighted by a jelly jar, on the table.

"Dear Mr. Drinkwater," it read, "there is cheese in the cupboard and bread and jam on the counter, under the dishcloth. Coffee's on the burner. I found your money, don't worry, it's safe. Be back around noon. Sincerely, Cally."

She'd found his money?

Goddamn it!

Had he been that drunk, that he'd hid it where she'd be certain to find it?

Well, yes, he had. He'd put it in the kitchen, the first place a woman went in the morning. Why the hell hadn't he stuck it in his sock or shoved it up into the sofa's cushions?

But she said it was safe. He just hoped that it wasn't safely in Big Mike's pocket.

Still grumbling, he sliced himself some bread and cheese and had breakfast, chasing it down with the pot of coffee, still hot on the stove top. It was pretty good coffee, too.

While he drank his last cup, he mentally laid out his plan for the day. From his quick glimpse of the register, he knew which room Toby was in.

If there was a different clerk on duty, he'd have no problem. If it was the same one, well, it was only one story up. He could circumvent the problem, climb up the outside of the building via the drainpipe, and have a look in the window.

He hoped the kid would be there. He wanted to catch up, trade stories, bring the boy up to date.

He put the money from his mind, which was no easy feat, slapped on his beaver hat, and set out for the Riverside Hotel.

It wasn't more than four blocks, and he sidled up to the front door and peeked around the corner. Different desk clerk. With a small sigh of relief, he walked on in, tipped his hat without a word, and proceeded up the stairs.

He found Toby's room with no difficulty and rapped at the door.

No answer.

Scowling, he knocked again, but was met with the same silence.

Looking both ways to make certain he was alone in the hallway, he dug into his pocket and pulled out a small length of wire that he kept for times such as this, and proceeded to insert it into the lock. Carefully, he turned it, and almost immediately he heard a click and felt the simple mechanism turn.

The door swung open.

Toby's bed hadn't been slept in. There were a few of Toby possessions scattered over the coverlet, though. One of those goddamn half-dime books—about Fargo, no less—a dime and a few pennies, and a half-eaten apple.

But no Toby.

He hadn't spent the night here, and suddenly Fargo was worried. What if the kid was lying dead in a ditch somewhere? He'd only had ten bucks on him, but ten dollars was enough money to get him rolled and murdered in this part of town.

A puzzled Fargo left the room just the way he'd found it, and slowly went down the stairs.

"Nobody home?" the clerk asked, although he barely glanced up from his newspaper.

"No," said Fargo. "Nobody."

He stood out front of the hotel for a few minutes, trying to decide on his next move. He could start scouring the streets and alleys for the kid, asking everybody he met if they'd seen a tall, dark-haired, blue-eyed kid. He could call in the cops. But both of those alternatives would defeat his purpose.

At last, he decided to just cool his heels. Toby's being gone all night wasn't a major calamity. After all, the boy had been living in the streets and alleys for two years.

Toby was smart.

Toby was streetwise.

At least, that's what Fargo told himself.

If he was going to find the boy—and Armstrong's goddamn ring, he couldn't forget that—then his best bet was to just hang around and keep his eyes open: business as usual for a confidence man like good old Larry Drinkwater from Des Moines.

He wished he hadn't chosen the first name, Larry, he thought as he walked back toward Cally's little row house. Spike, perhaps, or Snake. Now, that would have been better. It would have put a little fear into folks, he thought, at least, initially.

Larry conjured up no such sense of danger.

"Hey, Drinkwater!" bellowed a voice that could only belong to Big Mike Matthews.

Fargo looked across the street, and there he was, surrounded by several toughs. Toughs who either planned to befriend him and buy him a beer, or murder him and toss him in the river.

To a man they were all smiling, but Fargo knew that didn't make one whit of difference.

Big Mike waved a hand. "C'mon, Drinkwater! Meet the fellers!"

Fargo sighed.

He had a knife strapped to his leg and a derringer up his sleeve. He hoped to God that he wasn't going to have to use them. A machete and a cannon probably wouldn't be enough to take care of this little crowd of vipers.

Steeling himself for any contingency, Fargo waved back and started forward.

"Great!" he called. "Always glad to be met!"

He grinned wide.

10

"Lovely, my dear, just lovely!" Dawber said admiringly.

Frankly, Toby didn't feel the least bit "lovely." He felt like an idiot in the deep blue velvet suit and ruffled shirt. Ruffles at his cuffs, ruffles at his throat, and ruffles down his front. It was an advertisement for every tough within ten miles that said, "C'mon, beat me up!"

Plus which, the trousers hit him just below his knees and the cuffs were halfway to his elbows.

He couldn't even button the shirt, let alone the jacket.

Toby said, "I feel stupid. I look like a girl. An undressed girl! And I ain't gonna wear it."

Dawber continued smiling, but only with his lips. His eyes took on a hard glint. He said, "Yes, you are, my lovely. And don't say ain't. We are going to teach you the Queen's English, even if it kills you. Do you understand?"

"No."

Dawber shrugged. "It matters not a whit, dear Toby. You'll do it."

Toby had a sudden urge to just bolt and run. After all, he and Dawber were the only ones in the loft, and he'd lay money that he could beat Dawber to the door. But something kept his feet planted.

Perhaps it was the thought of Fargo, the great Fargo, out there counting on him.

Perhaps it was the money he'd make if he could just pull this off.

And maybe it was a little bit of fear, too, fear of Dawber finding him and killing him. Toby had known the bony old man only a short time, but in that span had decided that Dawber was just crazy enough to do it.

Whatever the reason, he just stood there and said, "Why? Why you got me rigged up like something out of a book? And I talk good enough English."

Dawber sighed. He rubbed his chin, considering. Just what it was that he was considering, Toby couldn't be sure. But then he looked up.

He said, "Sit down, lad."

"I can't," Toby said stubbornly. "I'll rip these here britches."

Dawber rolled his eyes and looked upward, as if to say *give me strength*. "All right," he said. "Change back into your own clothing and give those back to me, dearest."

Toby was awfully glad to hear those orders, and happily stripped to his butternuts, handed the fancy clothes over, and pulled on his regular duds.

Dawber folded the velvet outfit neatly, placed it on a crate, then sat beside it.

He waved a hand toward an opposite crate. "Sit, sit, my boy."

Toby sat and waited.

"Seventeen years ago, Mr. and Mrs. Wallings Beaufort had themselves a baby boy," Dawber began, "who was stolen in the night—by a disgruntled employee or a freelance agent, no one knows. To make a very long story short, no ransom was ever demanded, and the baby was never seen again. I—and the authorities—are of the opinion that it was killed and the body disposed of. However, this has not stopped Mrs. Beaufort from holding out hope."

Toby, who had become engrossed in the story, asked, "What about the Mister?"

"Dead," replied Dawber. "He died—heart attack—ten years ago."

"Okay, I feel bad for them," Toby allowed. He did, too. "I feel double bad for her. But what's this got to do with me?"

"Why, my darling child," Dawber said, rising to his feet, "you are their darling Teddy. Or will be, once I get you cleaned up and the rough edges smoothed away."

"Me?" Toby said. Or rather, squeaked. He couldn't keep his voice from breaking.

Suddenly, the possibility of death didn't seem so frightening. He imagined Mrs. Beaufort—fat and with a monocle and sitting on an angelic throne, practically—saying, "Come closer, boy."

Cripes.

And that poor little baby probably had a birthmark or something in a real embarrassing place. He didn't have any birthmarks himself, but he'd probably have to show her, anyway.

He said, "How you gonna convince her that I'm her baby, all growed up?"

"Dark, curly hair, blue eyes . . ." Dawber mused, more to himself than to Toby. He reached into a back pocket, pulled out a folded newspaper clipping, and handed it to Toby. "Mr. and Mrs. Beaufort," he said. "See any resemblance?"

Toby unfolded the clipping. It was old, and the pictures were drawings, but he believed he did bear a little resemblance to the late Mr. Beaufort. Of course, Beaufort was fat and old, but Toby thought he might have something like Beaufort's nose.

He touched his own, unconsciously.

Dawber laughed. "So you see?" he asked as he snatched back the clipping and folded it back into his pocket. "The lads have been searching for almost two years, now. You're the first who's made the grade. You should be proud, my boy."

"But how you gonna prove it's me?" asked Toby, thinking about birthmarks. "Hell, that kid could be anybody!"

"Indeed he could. But I intend to prove that it's you, and claim the reward for the long overdue return of Master Teddy Beaufort."

"And what do I get out of it?" Toby asked. Despite the remote possibility of this deal working out—and also despite his job with Fargo—he was curious. Beaufort sounded like a rich name.

"A lovely home, a doting mother, servants, a cook, and likely a few pretty young maidservants," Dawber said. "But most of all, you will receive upwards of seven hundred thousand upon your dear 'mama's' death. Which you will split with me, naturally," he added, and not as an afterthought.

Suddenly, Dawber's plan was sounding like a real winner. "Sure," Toby said softly. "Sure." It certainly beat the pee-wadding out of Fargo's lousy two hundred and fifty.

"Seven hundred thousand," he muttered. "Holy Christ."

Dawber smiled, and for once it went all the way up to his eyes. "Holy Christ, indeed."

Fargo had had about enough of this slapping-each-other-on-the-back shit. It seemed that once Big Mike said somebody was all right, he was all right with everybody in town. Or on the riverfront, at least.

Fargo hadn't heard so many amplified, blown-up stories of thievery and drunken tomfoolery since he was stuck up on the frozen Platte River with Buffalo Neck Tom Thurston for two weeks straight. He'd barely lived through that—and Buffalo Neck didn't know how close he'd come to taking a permanent dirt bath, either—and by God, Fargo wasn't about to let somebody get another start on chewing his ear off.

"Well," he said scraping his tavern chair back, "I hate to leave you boys, but I got a little business to take care of, if you know what I mean." To punctuate his point, he winked at Big Mike.

Big Mike nodded and said, "See you back at the

place, there, Drinkwater. You're company, and don't you forget it!"

Fargo took in a lungful of fresh air once he got outside. Even the stench of fish and human waste beat the atmosphere inside the tavern—stale beer, vomit, and ripe bodies—especially first thing in the morning when a man had drunk too much the night before.

Besides, it was almost noon. Time to get back to Cally's and see what the hell had happened to his money. He didn't forget to keep an eye out for Toby, though. He walked slowly through the crowded, noisy streets, searching the throng.

No luck.

He had a pang of worry, but quickly tamped it down, reminding himself that Toby wasn't exactly a babe in the woods. The worry didn't want to stay tamped, though.

It gnawed on him like a rat on a dead dog.

When he climbed the steps to Cally's stoop, he heard her singing before he even opened the door. He stood there a moment, listening to the soft, fluty song before he knocked.

The singing stopped and the door opened.

"Mr. Drinkwater!" she said, smiling. "You didn't need to knock. Nobody else does."

"My mama raised me to be polite, Miss Cally. And it's Drinkwater. No mister to it," he said taking off his hat as he walked inside. Christ, less than three minutes of her, and he was as hot as a pistol.

"And it's Cally, no miss," she said, grinning.

To cover the obvious bulge in his trousers, he went straight to the table and sat down in one of the chairs. Cally followed and went to the cupboard.

"You thirsty?" she asked, her backside swishing. "I just put the coffeepot on. Shouldn't be more than a few minutes."

"Fine," he said. "That'd be good. What'd you do with my money, Cally?"

He hadn't meant it to come out quite so harshly, but there you were.

But she didn't take offense. She turned to face him, swung one foot up on a chair, rucked up her dress to expose a shapely leg, and pulled his money pouch from her garter.

She tossed it on the tabletop and threw him a big smile.

"It's all there, in case you were wonderin'," she said, swinging her leg down. And, alas, her skirts.

"Course," she went on, "you can count it if you want. I just didn't want Mike findin' it. He'd tie you to an anvil and dump you in the river, sure as anything. And I don't want that to happen. I think I like you, Drinkwater."

Fargo believed that he might have blushed a little. "You do? Why, I'm sort of fond of you, too, Cally."

"That's fine," she said. "I'm glad." She turned around again and pulled down a sack of sugar from the cupboard. "But the main reason I didn't want Mike to toss you in the river is 'cause we got somethin' else cookin' in the stewpot, so to speak. I don't want him all of a sudden roaming around with all that cash. Might make some folks suspicious."

"Thanks," said Fargo. "I guess." What were she and Mike cooking up? He started to let his brain chew on that, then caught himself.

It didn't matter. He was after Armstrong's lucky ring. If he ever found Toby Jones again, dammit. And if the two of them could manage to locate Dawber which, so far, wasn't likely.

Cally laughed as she spooned sugar from a bag into the bowl on the table. "That Mike. Always takes six teaspoons of sugar in his coffee. He's about to eat us out of house and home."

She stopped spooning. "I didn't mean any offense, Drinkwater. About what I said about something else cooking, I mean. Like I said, I like you. You kinda grow on a person."

"Like a fungus?"

She laughed again. "Lord," she said, "you're sure a caution! You want some lunch to go with that coffee? I picked up some corned beef from Louie's on my way home. And Louie's place makes good corned beef. Lots of fat on it."

"That'd be fine," Fargo said. "Just fine."

Fargo watched with admiration as she moved about the kitchen, slicing the beef and the bread, pulling down a jar of pickled cucumbers and another of pickled eggs as well as a plate of butter, but he was distracted.

He continued to watch her as she moved to the stove, then back to the cupboards again, then back to the stove to pour out two mugs of steaming coffee.

What would her breasts look like, once he freed them? Would her legs be toned and sleek, would her waist be as tiny as it looked? He thought he might be able to clasp it with two hands.

But thoughts of Toby Jones kept intruding.

Where the hell was he?

11

"One more time, Toby darling."

Toby sighed. If he heard "one more time" one more time, he was going to hit somebody. Most probably Dawber, since he was the only other human in the place.

Of course, Dawber would likely pound him into the floorboards, face first. So he held off and repeated the list one more—and hopefully, last—time.

"I'm Toby Jones. I was raised in an orphanage in Kansas City, Missouri. I don't know where or when I was born, exactly. I was a baby when somebody left me on the stoop in a basket. Or so they tell me. The orphanage was pretty bad, but I stayed there until I turned fourteen or thereabouts, and then they turned me out. I just been wanderin' until I ran into Mr. Dawber, here," he paused to point at the man across from him, "and he thought I might be your son on account of the dates matching and all."

"And?" prompted Dawber.

"Oh. And because I'm left-handed, like your husband was, and because I've got dark hair. And it's kind of curly."

"Go on . . ."

"And because Mr. Dawber's been followin' your case," Toby added belatedly. "He's a real humanitarian, Mr. Dawber is."

"Very good," said Dawber with a smirking smile.

And Toby thought that it ought to be. It was all true.

Well, all except for the part about Dawber, anyhow.

"And then," Dawber went on, "I shall point out your dark blue eyes, so like the late Mr. Beaufort's, and the shape of your chin and your nose, also like Mr. Beaufort's, and your mouth, like Mrs. Beaufort's late father."

Dawber paused. "Naturally, your mouth isn't anything like Mrs. Beaufort's father's, but we shall count on those dark good looks of yours to carry the day. That, and the fact that you can, indeed be traced back to that orphanage. And the birth dates will be similar."

"But I don't know when I was—" Toby began.

Dawber waved his hands. "I told you, my boy. It doesn't matter. The date you were taken in is all that will matter, and you were taken in after the Beaufort baby was stolen."

Toby asked, "And that's it? You mean, you think she's gonna believe this? She's been looking for her kid for fifteen years or thereabouts. There's likely been a string of folks tryin' to sell her on this boy or that boy."

He didn't mean to fight Dawber. After all, he didn't want a repeat of that throttle business. He just should have agreed with everything the man said in the hopes that he'd go out and leave him alone for a while. All he needed was a chance to slip into Dawber's "room" and take a look for that damned ring!

But he couldn't resist taking a poke at what the Old Man back at the orphanage would have called "circular logic."

"Ah," Dawber said. "You're thinking, aren't you, my pretty?"

He stood up and his expression changed, suddenly darkening. "Do us all a favor, my dear Toby. Don't think. That will be my department. Do you understand me?"

Toby gritted his teeth, but he said, "Yes sir."

Dawber's expression turned sunny again, the cloud

passing as suddenly as it had come. "Excellent! And how clever of you to be left-handed. It's a marvelous touch, you know."

Toby said nothing. But he did what he always did when something or somebody was ticking him off—he made the odd but mostly unremarkable action of turning his fingers under, then grinding his knuckles on the arm of his chair.

The Old Man and his minions back at the home had warned him that he'd stunt his hand that way, but he hadn't listened, and it hadn't grown stunted.

Screw them, anyway. Showed how much *they* knew.

"Well," Dawber said, walking into his quarters, "we could both use a brief respite from this." There came to Toby's ears a series of scraping sounds, like crates being moved, and wood being pried up, then hammered back down again.

"And yes," Dawber shouted over the din, "I know you're hungry. I can hear your stomach growling from here."

Then the sounds stopped, and Dawber came back out into the main room. Belatedly, he stuck a little pouch into his pocket, which Toby assumed contained spending money.

"When I return," he continued, walking toward the exit, "we shall do something about your hair. I can't take you to meet your 'mother' with you looking like a ragamuffin, now can I?"

Toby thought that perhaps Dawber could use a visit to the barber—and another to a haberdasher—more than he could, but wisely kept his mouth shut tight. He just nodded.

"And don't fret, lad," said the walking skeleton. "I'll bring you back something to eat."

Dawber stepped through the door, and Toby heard the click of the key on the lock behind him. Dawber was taking no chances on Toby's running off, then. Even if he found the ring, where could he hide it when he couldn't get outside?

"Damn it," Toby grumbled, and crept to the door,

pressing his ear against it, listening for the sound of Dawber's receding footsteps on the stairs.

When he was certain Dawber had gone down at least two flights, he tiptoed carefully back toward Dawber's partitioned room, paused a few seconds just to make sure, then slipped inside.

Then slipped right out again, muttering, "Jesus, it's darker than the inside of a black sow in there!"

He fetched a candle and lit it off one of the many burning in the attic. Then he went back, idly wondering if Dawber intended to keep him up here until he'd grown white as a ghost. He missed the sun.

He placed the candle atop an upended crate, then got to work. If he were Dawber, where would he keep his treasure?

Well, he might as well start working his way around the room. He dug a penny from his pocket and flipped it high into the air, catching it on the back of his hand. It came up heads. Left to right, then.

He opened the first trunk.

Dawber made his way down the street, content in the knowledge that at this very moment, young Toby was more than likely rifling his room.

Well, let him. He was new, and all the boys—filthy scamps—did it when they first came, and at the very first chance they got. Dawber had made sure that Toby got his chance earlier than most.

Dawber, for the moment carrying everything of value that he owned—pinned into the lining of his long coat, the hems of his trousers and his shirt, hidden in secret pockets and stuffed into the inner band of his hat—began to hum as he walked. He was oblivious to the way the crowd parted before him, the manner in which some backed away.

Well, not totally oblivious. But he thought it was on account of his compelling physical appearance.

He had been quite a good-looking man, once upon a time. But that had been long ago, when he was young, before his family—and the constabulary—had shipped him off to the colonies out of shame. That he still pictured himself this way—young, handsome, and full of pluck—was not unusual. He was, after all, human.

What he didn't take into account was that he now was only a shadow of his former robust, handsome self. He had become rail thin, his features had turned into a caricature of sin, and his hair, once his crowning glory, was thinning and wispy.

He also smelled rather gamey, even to these pathetic denizens of the docks and the riverfront.

But as he walked along with a little bounce in his step, he felt, on the inside, that he was a handsome man, a witty man, an intelligent man who was wealthy, and about to be much, much wealthier.

Fargo had walked up and down the length and breadth of the St. Louis riverfront—at least, the seedy part of it—three times since leaving Cally. He was more worried about Toby than ever: so worried, in fact, that it had momentarily pushed Cally from his thoughts.

He was wondering if the kid was in serious trouble of some kind. And the Lord knew there were plenty of kinds of trouble for him to get into. Plenty of ways for a boy on his own to die.

Fargo had searched the faces in the crowds, all right, but he'd also kept an eye peeled for any unusual, human-shaped humps in the alleys. He found a couple, but they were only drunks.

So what had happened to the kid?

He'd been back to Toby's hotel, but just once more. He didn't want to raise suspicions. The room was just as he'd found it the last time. No trace of an occupant, except for the few objects carelessly tossed on the coverlet. They were in the same places as last time. Toby hadn't been back.

Toby, it seemed, hadn't been anywhere.

Fargo walked down one of the docks, toward a small cargo boat. Stopping halfway out, he sat down on a barrel to think. As the muddy water flowed beneath him, carrying silt from Minnesota and Iowa and

Illinois on its journey to the Gulf of Mexico, he decided to give Toby one more day.

If the kid was dead, one day wouldn't matter one way or the other. But if he was alive, and if he was on to something, it might make all the difference in the world.

But . . . dead.

That single word bothered Fargo more than he'd like to admit. He hadn't known the boy all that long, and lads of that age had drawn on him before, and died for it. But he felt that Toby was a good kid inside, despite the manner of their meeting.

He was a kid that just needed a chance.

And I gave him one, all right, Fargo thought bitterly. *I gave him a chance to get himself murdered on some dark, damp street.*

Fargo realized he'd forgotten something that he promised himself he'd never forget: he'd taken the whole thing for a game. And that's where he'd tripped himself up. Everything out here on the frontier was deadly serious, with the emphasis on deadly. And now it may have cost an innocent boy his life.

No, not it. Him.

He stood up. Watching this water run was making him get all moody. Maybe he had taken the ring and the kid too lightly.

All right, maybe he had taken the whole damn thing too lightly. He'd just come off a job of serious bounty hunting that very nearly got him killed three times, and compared to that, finding Armstrong's bauble had seemed like a picnic.

But it wasn't.

Not for Armstrong, not for Fargo, and surely not for Toby.

He made his way back up the dock to solid ground again, then hied himself up the hill, to the streets and the crowds.

He could look for Toby a couple more times before it got dark.

Dammit, anyway!

12

Nervously playing with the beaded fringe on her handbag, Cally, in her best, most subdued dress, sat in the large, elegant, flower-filled parlor of Mrs. Wallings Beaufort.

Big Mike had made her come. It had been all his idea. And he should have been the one to do the dirty work, not her.

At least, that's the way she saw it.

But Big Mike was a lot stronger than she was and hit a lot harder, and so she was here, feeling a bit like she was going to lose her lunch at any second.

There came a scrape as the double doors slid open, and Cally got to her feet and nervously smoothed her hair. A butler—the first she had ever seen outside of a picture in a novel—announced, "Mrs. Beaufort, Miss Calista Teach," as he moved to the side, allowing a well-dressed older woman into the room. Bowing, he stepped out and closed the doors behind him.

The woman, Mrs. Beaufort, had no smile for Cally. She simply regarded her and said, "You wished to see me. Something about my son, I believe."

"Yes, ma'am," Cally began. "See, I live down at the docks, and a couple days ago—"

The old woman held up a weary hand. "Stop, young woman. If this is yet another attempt to foist some young imposter off on me, save your breath. My son is dead. Long dead."

That brought Cally up short. For a moment, she

was stuck for something to say, then blurted, "No, ma'am, he isn't! I think we found him! Honest!"

This, in turn, took Mrs. Beaufort by surprise. After a moment of silence, she motioned to the sofa. "Sit, child," she said.

Once Cally was seated, and Mrs. Beaufort, too, the older of the women said, "Now, what in the world makes you very certain of this, Miss . . ."

"Teach. Calista Teach. But everybody calls me Cally."

"Very well. Cally, then. What makes you so very certain?"

"Mrs. Beaufort," Cally said, leaning forward, hands clasped, "I remember when your son was taken. I remember my mama being all upset about it. It was in all the papers and everybody talked, you know?"

Mrs. Beaufort sighed. "Yes. I know better than most."

Cally raced ahead. "So I've always been, whatyoucall . . . aware of it. Anyhow, a couple days ago, there was this kid down on the docks. He put me in mind of somebody, 'cept I couldn't figure out who it was. And then it came to me, right out of the clear blue sky. It was your husband, Mrs. Beaufort. He was the spittin' image."

Mrs. Beaufort simply arched a brow.

Oh, you're a tough nut to crack, aren't you? Cally thought. But she moved ahead anyway.

"See, there's this man," Cally continued. "This man named Dawber. He runs a bunch of kids down on the docks. Pickpocketry and purse thieving and the like."

"How distasteful," muttered Mrs. Beaufort with a little sniff.

"Yes, ma'am, he's a real distasteful feller. And the thing is, he's got this kid, the one I was just tellin' you about. Me and my friend, Mike, we're afraid that he's gonna try to bamboozle you. You know, pick up a big chunk of change on the kid. And me and Mike, we don't think that's right. 'Cept we can't get the kid away from him. He's got him locked up."

"My dear," said Mrs. Beaufort, seeming much more bored than a woman should be, who has just been told that her long-lost son is in grave peril, "just what is all this to me? I'm sorry for this child, and I'm appalled at this Mr. Dibber's actions—"

"Dawber."

"Dawber. But alas, my son is dead. There is no reward. I have washed my hands of plots and conspiracies that derive sustenance from an old woman's hope."

She stood up, and Cally did, too. "And now, if you will excuse me," said Mrs. Beaufort, "I have an appointment."

"But Mrs. Beaufort!"

"Thank you for calling, my dear, but don't come again. James?"

As if by magic, the doors slid open and the butler appeared. Mrs. Beaufort slipped out of the door and the butler nodded to Cally. "This way, miss."

She picked up her handbag and went through the door, but before she was all the way down the front entry hall, she turned and said, "You tell her something for me. You tell her I'll bet my boots that the kid in trouble is her boy. Big Mike and me are gonna try to get our hands on him by ourselves, if she won't help, and bring him up here. And she'd better take a look at him, if she knows what's good for her."

The butler raised his brows. "Is that a threat, miss?"

"Threat? No, no. It's a . . . well, just tell her, all right? And tell her there's more to the story, if she'd only listen."

The butler went around her and opened the front door. It was very fancy, with intricately etched glass panes surrounded by fine wood. Probably mahogany, Cally thought.

That door had probably cost more than she made in a whole damned year.

The butler ushered her through with a nod of his head and another "miss," and before she knew it, she was out on the wide front porch with the door closed behind her.

The thing was that Mike and Dawber had been talking over this for a long time now: how they'd find a kid that fit the Beaufort boy's description, one about the right age, and then try to sell him to Mrs. Beaufort.

Well, not sell him exactly, but get themselves a nice reward. Dawber'd had his boys looking for a likely candidate for months and months. Years, actually.

Cally suspected that Dawber would arrange another taste for himself, likely from the boy's inheritance when the old lady kicked off. Which Dawber would probably have a hand in.

She wouldn't put it past him, not one bit.

She had heard more than they thought she had. When she was there, they always acted like she wasn't, except when they needed another cup of coffee or another shot or something.

There was a great deal of advantage, sometimes, to being invisible.

Especially when she had hoped to do one good thing, to maybe make up for all the bad things she'd done in her life. She was going to go up to Mrs. Beaufort's all right, but she wasn't going to say what Big Mike had told her to. No. She'd planned to lay all her cards out on the table. She'd tell the truth, and the hell with Big Mike.

Except that hadn't been a very good plan, had it? Mrs. Beaufort didn't believe her anyway and hadn't even let her get to the good part, the part about how she wanted to double-cross even Big Mike, and turn the kid over for free, no strings.

But the old biddy had practically tossed her out on her ear, and now she'd be in Dutch with Mike and Dawber. If they found out what she'd done—or, what she planned to do—which they surely would. Dawber was like that. He was practically a soothsayer, always figuring out a person's secrets.

Not that it would cut any ice with Dawber that Mike

had told her that they were going to cut Dawber out. And he'd showed her the razor in his pocket. In this case, when Mike said cut, he meant it literally.

Right now, she could practically feel that razor at her own throat instead of Dawber's. Oh, she'd messed things up, messed them up good.

At last, she made her feet move, and slowly walked down to the street. Trudging toward the cross street, where she could flag down a cab, it suddenly hit her. Mr. Larry Drinkwater.

He seemed a nice enough fellow. Oh, she'd seen his eyes, seen the way they followed her around. She knew what he wanted. But then, wasn't that just part of being a man? And wasn't the knowing of it just part of being a woman?

The thing was that he'd never done anything about it. Never even tried to hire her for an hour. That's what made all the difference in the world. He wanted her, but he respected her enough to see, at least, that she was Big Mike's woman.

That she didn't want to be Big Mike's, that she was desperately seeking to become anybody's woman *but* Big Mike's, was beside the point.

Or perhaps it was the point.

Hell, she'd be Drinkwater's woman in a slap second if he would only ask, and she wouldn't charge him for the privilege, either. And he probably wouldn't make her work the streets.

Suddenly, a spring came into her step. There was a way out of this, perhaps. It was as twisted as a corkscrew, but maybe—just maybe—she could make it work.

Humming, she walked on.

"Cally?" Big Mike said, trying to act natural. The crowd in the Little Cougar was loud, but not as boisterous as it would be later in the evening. "Don't know. Probably in an alley somewhere with some river rat. What you doin' down here, anyway?"

"Prowling," Dawber replied cryptically. "Just a little prowling." He raised a hand and caught the bartender's eye. "Beer," he said, then added to Mike, "I'll never get used to beer so long as I live. I don't understand why a person can't get a nice pint of stout in this ridiculous country."

Big Mike had no answer for that. He was just satisfied to have diverted Dawber's attention away from Cally's whereabouts. Big Mike prided himself on being a good liar—a great liar!—but Dawber knew him well enough to catch him in a lie in a second.

And Dawber wasn't very nice when he thought people were lying to him.

At least, he hadn't been too nice to Mugston Ross when Mugston lied to him last year. Mugston simply disappeared one night. Just gone, just like that. And when Mike had asked Dawber about it, Dawber had just smiled.

That smile still gave Big Mike the colly wobbles, even after a whole year.

It was the same smile that had been plastered over Dawber's face when Tony Gordon disappeared, and when they'd found Robbie Ames strapped to the paddle wheel of a big riverboat, dead as a doornail and already half picked clean by the fish and crawdads.

Big Mike didn't want to end up on the downside of a paddle wheel riverboat, like old Robbie.

Just act real casual, he told himself, and smiled at the man across the table. *Just keep Dawber happy, and the second you pull this deal off, it's a new town and a new name for you.*

"How's the kid?" he asked offhand. At least, he hoped it appeared that way.

Big Mike had planned to take Cally with him when he skipped town, but lately, he was setting his mind against it. It was easier to track two people traveling together than it was a single man, especially if that man changed his name and his trade and didn't flash his newly gotten cash around too much.

Maybe he'd take Cally with him for a while, just to confuse things. He could always dump her later.

No, best to do away with her. If she was alive, she could be found, and if she could be found, she could get Dawber that much closer to finding him.

"The boy is fine," Dawber said. He sipped at his beer, then made a face. "The boy is better than fine, actually. I couldn't have wished for a better one. He even has some resemblance to Beaufort. Quite amazing, really."

"All the better," Mike said, staring out the front window. It was best not to look at Dawber directly. Somehow, the bastard knew when you were keeping something from him, and right now Mike was about to burst. Where the hell was Cally, anyway? What had happened up in the mansion district with Old Lady Beaufort?

"Is there something wrong, my friend," Dawber asked, and in his voice, Big Mike read suspicion.

But just then, he saw his salvation. "Say, Dawber, there's somebody I'd like you to meet! Hang on a minute, will ya?" Big Mike bolted from the corner table, out the door, and slapped a paw on Larry Drinkwater's shoulder.

Drinkwater jumped and whirled to face him, his expression relaxing when he saw who was manhandling him. "Mike!" Drinkwater said. "You about scared the liver out of me!"

"Sorry, chum," Mike said. He'd never been so relieved to see anybody in his life. Actually, he would have been just as happy if it had been anybody that Dawber didn't know. He just needed an excuse to change the subject, and quickly.

Drinkwater was a dream come true.

He threw an arm around Drinkwater's shoulders. "C'mon, Drinkwater! In here. There's somebody I want you to meet."

Cally paid the cabby, then walked down to the docks, where the cabby wouldn't go. And once again, she thought that it was terrible to live and work in a place even the hacks and cabs were afraid to enter.

She walked down toward the river, the odor of it rising with every step, and at last put her hand on the door to the Little Cougar, where she was supposed to meet Big Mike.

She wasn't looking forward to it. Even though Mrs. Beaufort hadn't let her get to her secret plan, she'd thrown her out, and before she could even tell her all of *Mike's* plan.

He wasn't going to like that. He wasn't going to like that at all.

She was glad she was to meet him in a public place, even though Mike considered the Little Cougar about the same as her parlor. Maybe he wouldn't knock her around quite so much in front of people. Maybe, for once, he'd be kind.

But she doubted it.

So she opened the door of the Little Cougar, took a step inside, then just as quickly stepped right back out and ducked around the corner. She was fairly certain that nobody had seen her.

Dawber was in there, in the flesh, talking with Big Mike.

And if there was one thing she couldn't deal with right at this moment, it was Big Mike *and* Dawber.

She turned on her heel, once she got her stomach back in place, and went home.

13

Sweating and out of breath, a dejected Toby sat on the floor just outside of Dawber's quarters, which he'd just finished methodically searching for the second time.

Every pin and needle had been put meticulously back in place—twice—every shoe, every shirt (both of them); every scrap of cloth and leather, metal, wood and glass; and every secret sweet had been carefully moved, looked under, looked behind, and in some cases looked inside of.

Twice.

And at last, Toby had to face the fact that if there was a treasure hoard, even a tiny one, it wasn't in Dawber's room. He'd even rapped the floorboards, searching for a loose plank, a missing nail, anything, and had come up empty.

Could Fargo have been wrong? The idea hadn't crossed his mind until just this moment. After all, Fargo was a famous man! And why would Fargo make the whole thing up, anyway?

Try as he might, Toby couldn't imagine a single scenario for which spinning a tall tale about somebody named Armstrong and a stolen ring would have been appropriate.

Or necessary.

Or even mildly useful.

No, it wasn't Fargo. Fargo, he decided, had been

straight with him. Fargo had given him ten dollars, hadn't he? Trusted him to come on into town, all by himself. And besides, he just had a good feeling about Fargo.

So it had to be Dawber. Now, Dawber wasn't the sort to trust banks or safety deposit boxes. Even after less than twenty-four hours of making his acquaintance, Toby was sure of that.

So he must have the stuff on him. Therefore, it had to be a small stash. Of what, exactly, Toby wasn't sure. All he knew was that there was a red ruby ring in the mix, for the return of which Fargo would pay him two hundred and fifty dollars.

As to the rest?

Well, maybe he didn't need to tell Fargo about that. Maybe he'd just keep that his little secret. He imagined his pockets clinking with cash and jewels as he rode out of town, and he smiled.

And speaking of Dawber's secrets, just where had this Mrs. Beaufort thing come from, anyway? He knew Fargo hadn't known about it. He sort of figured that Fargo would have mentioned a little detail like that.

If he had to repeat his life story for Dawber one more lousy time, he figured he'd go stark raving lunatic mad.

Right now, he suddenly realized, his most immediate problem was getting out of the attic. Not that he planned to run away or anything foolish like that.

He just had to take a piss.

He unfolded his long legs and stood up, pulled his drying shirt away from his body and gave it a little shake, then walked down to the far end of the room to the door.

There, he tryed the latch, although he'd heard Dawber lock it from the outside. No luck. So he pulled up a crate and sat down.

And waited, with nervously crossed legs, for somebody to come.

*   *   *

Fargo found himself being hurried through the front door of the Little Cougar Café—and right into the arms of none other than Randall Dawber, in the flesh! After all, who could mistake that skeletal form, that stringy white hair, that vulpine look?

He almost gawked, he was that surprised, but managed to get a grip on himself.

"Dawber!" Big Mike roared jovially. "This here's my new buddy Drinkwater. Larry Drinkwater, meet my old pal, Dawber."

Fargo extended his hand and Dawber took it briefly, giving it a half-hearted and not-too-firm shake. Fargo noticed that he didn't stand.

Big Mike went to the next table and jerked the chair right out from under a patron. He twirled it around and offered it to Fargo who moved back—the patron who had just lost the chair was none too happy. But when he saw it was Big Mike who had unseated him, he simply backed off.

Interesting, thought Fargo with a hoisted brow, and took the chair. Big Mike scraped his out, too, and they sat down with Dawber.

"Two beers!" Big Mike hollered over the throng. Then he picked up his mug and drained the last drops from it. "What you been up to today, Drinkwater?"

"Just walkin' around," Fargo answered. He didn't have to lie. "Some kind of town you got here."

"That it is, that it is," Big Mike answered much too jovially, and slapped Fargo on the back.

Fargo pitched forward at the impact, but kept his seat. He even managed a laugh.

Dawber just sat there, nursing his beer.

Which left Fargo to wonder what had happened just before he came on the scene. Had Big Mike and Dawber had a falling out, or was Big Mike trying to distract Dawber from something? Mike was being overly friendly, that was for certain.

It didn't matter, at least, not for the moment. Right now, Fargo just thanked his lucky stars that Dawber and Big Mike were acquainted at all, and that he had owned the luck to gain an introduction this soon. It was beyond his hopes.

Except, now that he had an introduction, he wondered what to do with it. This was a stroke of fate he hadn't counted on, let alone considered.

"Dawber," Big Mike went on as their beers were delivered, "Drinkwater, here, he's from up Des Moines way."

Fargo nodded. "There, and other places. Been around some." He hoisted his beer and took a gulp. Actually, it tasted pretty good even if it was warm, mostly because his hangover from last night had at last worn off, and because he'd been out in the sun all day.

Dawber spoke at last. One brow hoisted, he said, "Really. Where have you been? We locals crave tales of exciting places, you know."

Dawber's every word dripped with sarcasm, but Big Mike didn't seem to notice, so Fargo pretended to be dumb, too. He said, "Oh, all over Iowa and Minnesota. Spent some time out in Nebraska, around Omaha. Even was down in the Indian Territory once upon a time. But mostly, up in St. Paul."

"My, my," said Dawber, not the least bit impressed.

Fargo held back the inclination to slug him.

"Drinkwater's in the same business we are," Big Mike went on. And then he elbowed Fargo in the ribs. "Ain't that right, Drinkwater?"

Fargo lifted his mug again and studied Dawber over its rim. "I don't know. I don't believe Mr. Dawber's stated his business yet."

Dawber's expression flicked briefly into something that Fargo found very unsettling, then changed back to apathy again just as quickly. He stood up. "I must be going, gentlemen. Good day."

He shot a meaningful gaze at Big Mike before he nodded at Fargo, and then he left. Fargo had read that look he'd given Mike, though. It said, "Shut the hell up" in no uncertain terms.

He watched the door swing closed behind Dawber, then said, "I interrupt somethin'?"

Big Mike, suddenly irritable, scowled and said, "No. Nothin' at all." He took a swig of his beer. "You got a lot of nerve, askin' Dawber his business."

"Didn't mean anything by it," Fargo said innocently.

"Yeah, well," grumbled Big Mike. "You seen Cally this afternoon?"

"Not since I left your place," Fargo said. "And by the way, that was real square of you to let me stay the night."

"Sure," Mike said, distracted. He stared past Fargo and out the front windows. "Sure, any time. I mean that."

"You do? Seriously? Cause if you do, I'd admire to impose on your hospitality a little longer. Just till I get my feet under me, you understand."

Without preamble, Big Mike shot to his feet and knocked over his chair in the process. "There she is, the little guttersnipe!" He bulled his way to the door and outside. Fargo turned to see him grabbing Cally—dressed really nice, Fargo thought—by the arm and jerk her around, hard.

Fargo nearly raced after him on pure instinct. Nobody should treat Cally like that.

No man should treat any woman like that.

But something held him back, and that thing was the thought of Toby.

And so he hesitated. Just long enough that Big Mike let go of Cally.

Fargo let out a whistling sigh through his teeth. Big Mike didn't know how close he'd come to dying. Well, at least getting his ass whipped pretty damned good. Fargo vowed right then and there that once he got this thing with Toby cleared up to his satisfaction, he was going to get Cally away from Big Mike, get her away and help her get set up someplace new, someplace that didn't stink of fish and garbage or Big Mike Matthews.

Someplace nice.

She deserved it.

Now Big Mike and Cally were just standing there, talking. Through the window, Fargo saw Cally gesture with her hands, as if she were trying to explain something, something she was a little hesitant to tell.

Then Big Mike's face clouded over and he raised a fist. But not to strike her. Angrily, he shook it off toward town, as if he were cursing the city.

Very strange, thought Fargo. *Just what the hell is that son of a bitch up to?*

The key turned in the lock, and Toby jumped up, hopping from foot to foot.

Dawber's head emerged from the opening door, and Toby shouted, " 'Scuse me!" as he fairly shoved Dawber out of the way and bolted down the stairs.

He heard Dawber's footsteps following him, but paid them no mind. He wanted to find the closest window in a big hurry.

Sighing, he finally relieved himself into the alley, two floors below.

"I knew you wouldn't run away, my boy," said Dawber's voice, behind him.

Toby buttoned his britches, then turned around. "You were gone for an awful long time," he said angrily. "You should'a left me a key or somethin'. I'm not some little kid who has to ask permission to go to the outhouse, you know."

Dawber smiled, and then it passed. He said, "Come back upstairs, my dear. I've brought you some food. I've brought supper for us all."

Toby didn't move. "Us all? There's just you and me here."

Just then, he heard distant clatter from below: feet climbing stairs. Was it that time already?

Dawber turned away and started toward the staircase, saying, "Not for long, my dear. Listen! Even now my lovely brood returns from their day's labors. Hear their tiny bootsteps upon the treads?"

Toby sighed. Here he was—starving to death, for

cripe's sake, with his bladder practically exploding, under the care of a madman with unknown treasure stuffed into his pockets.

And Toby was doing this for only two hundred and fifty dollars?

And then he remembered just what a man could do with two hundred and fifty. He supposed he could stand a little more strangeness.

He might even put up with having to cross his legs real hard for an hour again, too.

Or the next time, he might just go piss in Dawber's bed linens.

That would teach the creepy old bastard.

The heads of the first boys became visible, rising up the stairs from the lower floor, and he joined them as they marched up the next flight, listening to their chatter as they compared their spoils.

One had ten dollars and a lady's ring, another had a watermelon. Three dollars here, a purse with a few pennies there; a pilfered topcoat, a cheap bracelet, a loaf of bread, still hot: maybe Dawber wasn't so crazy after all.

14

Fargo had said good-bye to Big Mike and Cally quickly. Although he hated to just walk off and leave Cally with Mike, he had to get on Dawber's tail as soon as possible.

He sauntered out of Big Mike and Cally's sight casually, after saying he'd meet them back at Cally's place for supper. Once clear, he lit a fire under his own boots. Dodging and darting, he went in the direction that he'd seen Dawber walk off, and sure enough, he caught sight of him at last.

Dawber, his thin frame and long, wispy, white hair unmistakable from any distance, was just emerging from a butcher shop. He carried a brown-wrapped package under his arm.

Fargo followed him down another block, where Dawber stepped into a small greengrocer's. A few minutes later, he came out with another parcel.

Fargo kept on following, hanging back in the crowds until the crowds started to thin. Then he moved from alley to doorway, from trash bin to stoop.

As the long shadows of dusk darkened the streets, Dawber came into a relatively deserted area, and disappeared into a darkened building marked with a NO TRESPASSING sign, which he ignored.

Fargo slid into the mouth of an alley across the way, sat himself down on a pile of discarded timbers, and waited.

He didn't have to wait long before something happened, although it wasn't what he expected.

He'd expected Dawber to emerge again, probably with some new package, and move on. But instead, boys started to come: over a dozen of them, in groups of twos and threes, one carrying a watermelon, one carrying a man's overcoat nearly as big as he was.

Fargo watched as they all made their way down the street, turned in at the NO TRESPASSING sign, and ducked into the building.

No lights were lit that he could see, though night was falling fast. Where on earth could they have gone? And then it struck him: the attic.

Of course. What better place for a man to disappear into with all those children, to remain unseen, than a windowless attic in a deserted part of town?

He began watching the roofline, and sure enough, within twenty minutes a thin, barely visible plume of smoke began to rise from a chimney he couldn't see from this vantage.

Dawber was whipping up some supper for his boys.

How sweet.

How goddamn homey.

Fargo ground his teeth. More than likely, Toby was up there. This thought both pleased and enraged him. If it were true, he was thankful that something unknown hadn't happened to the boy—that he hadn't gotten rolled and beaten senseless, or that he wasn't lying dead in some alley.

But on the other hand, now that he'd met Dawber, he couldn't imagine a less likely candidate to shepherd young boys through their formative years.

He watched the thin smoke lifting skyward until it was completely dark. And then, at last, he moved on. He just wished that Toby would lay his hands on that damn ring quickly, then get the hell out of there.

In one piece.

"Don't make me recite you the whole thing again, please!" Cally said. She was at the stove, cooking cabbage to go with the corned beef she'd purchased earlier that day.

"I told you twice, every word," she went on, wearily. "She wouldn't believe me, all right? She practically had me thrown into the street. By her goddamn butler!"

"Well, you're sure dressed for it," Mike growled sarcastically.

"I'm dressed nice!" she said, waving a wooden spoon, dripping with cabbage, at him. "This is the best dress I got."

"Needs more beads," Mike grumped. "Needs more goddamn somethin'. How could you mess it up like that? I told you what to say. You must not have said it good, or said it right, else she wouldn't have tossed you on your ear. Now what are we gonna do? You got any smart ideas for that?"

She sighed. At least he hadn't hit her.

Yet.

She took a chance. She said, "I don't know, Mike. You're the brain. You figure it out."

It was too much.

In a split second he had crossed the room and slammed her up against the wall. She tried to scream, but no sound came out. He had her by the throat, half strangling her, and she couldn't catch her breath.

His face inches from hers, he growled, "Don't you sass me, you stinkin' bitch. You're the one what loused us up. Probably loused up Dawber's deal, too, and don't you think for a slap second that he's gonna be as forgivin' as me."

The room started to go all dizzy and dim, and Cally felt herself losing consciousness, felt herself sliding away . . .

Then suddenly she dropped to the floor, landing in a heap beside the stove. And at the same moment in which she slipped to earth and back toward consciousness, she heard a roar and a loud pop.

Mike cried out in pain and rage, and then somebody threw a chair. Even in her dazed state, she knew it was a chair, because it broke and splintered against the wall above and to her right, and one of the broken spindles landed in her lap.

Amid the whirling shouts and thudding sounds of fists hitting flesh, she picked it up dully and tried to focus on it.

And while she was making the many fuzzy images coalesce into one clear one, Drinkwater suddenly landed in her lap.

"Mr. Drinkwater?" she said stupidly, even as he hauled himself up and wordlessly threw himself back into the fight.

She was pretty sure there was blood trickling down his face.

And then it all came rushing in on her. Drinkwater had come in and seen Mike choking her, and this was the result.

She tried to climb to her feet but fell back, and her first thought was that this was the first time in her life that a man had fought for her. Not over her—that was different—but *for* her.

Her second thought, falling quickly on the footsteps of the first, was to stop it and stop it fast. She'd seen Mike cripple one man in a barroom fight and kill a second. They had both been huge men, bigger than Drinkwater. And she wanted to keep Drinkwater around.

Again, she pulled herself up just as Drinkwater's punch knocked Big Mike across the table. It broke with his weight and he crashed to the floor.

Mike shook his head like a wet dog, and roared, "You stinkin' shit! I took your lousy ass in off the street! I gave you a place to sleep and hang your hat!"

And Big Mike leapt up anew, faster than she had suspected a man of his size could leap.

Drinkwater, the blood now streaming down his face, moved in again, shouting, "And now I'm gonna toss your ass out, you stupid son of a bitch!"

Big Mike landed a blow to Drinkwater's shoulder,

while Drinkwater ducked and punched Mike in the gut, and Cally screamed, "Stop it! Stop it!"

She might as well have whispered "stop" to a pair of freight trains.

Mike staggered back a few feet. Drinkwater lowered his head and butted his opponent in the stomach as hard as he could. At least, he grunted from the effort.

But Mike wasn't admired and feared on the docks for nothing. Although the breath was nearly knocked from him, he dropped back another few feet, almost to the wall, then suddenly charged forward, grabbed Drinkwater around the waist, and hurled him across the room.

Drinkwater landed against her mother's bureau with a grunt of pain, cracking the top drawers, and Cally gasped. Not for the bureau, but for Drinkwater.

Drinkwater slid to the floor as Big Mike made his move: he pulled a lethal-looking blade from the top of his boot and started for Drinkwater.

Cally didn't hesitate. She leapt on Mike's back, clinging to him like a jockey to a draft horse. One hand was wrapped around his neck, the other tore at his hair. Her knees dug into his sides, and she shouted, "Stop it, Michael Matthews! You stop it this instant, you hear me, Mike?"

He paused long enough to shout, "Get off, woman!" but it was long enough.

Drinkwater was up once again. Cally saw his gaze flick to the knife in Mike's hand just before he said, "Oh, you want to play that game, do you?"

"Mike . . ." she said, her voice filled with warning, although not so much for Big Mike as for Drinkwater, who was unarmed.

Or was he?

Where he'd found it she did not know, but when she looked back at Drinkwater there was a blade in his hand, too: a blade larger and more deadly than Mike's.

It was the kind she'd heard called an Arkansas Toothpick, serrated and wicked.

Suddenly—and belatedly—Cally's sense of self-preservation took over. She slid to the floor and scuttled back into the corner while Mike and Drinkwater stood there, staring daggers at each other, panting raggedly.

"Please," she whispered. "Please stop it." She barely heard her own words.

And then Mike laughed.

Cally cocked her head.

Mike laughed big and loud, from his belly, and hollered, "Goddamn it, Drinkwater, you've got a lot of bark on you! Beats everything I ever seen, you know that?"

And Drinkwater seemed to relax, too. His blue eyes, which had gone dark and stormy in his anger, lightened a little. His stance relaxed.

And Cally saw her chance.

She got up, brushed her skirts off, planted hands on her hips, said a quick, silent prayer, and said, as crankily as she could, "Jesus Christ! Just look at what you boys have done to my front room with all your rowdy-dow! I swan, I ought to take the broom to the both of your backsides!"

It worked.

Drinkwater finally broke out in a guffaw, and Big Mike turned away from him to toss Cally a grin and a horselaugh.

Cally shook her head. And then she shook her finger. "You two help me get this place cleaned up, you hear? And no more horseplay in the house!"

You had to admire her, Fargo thought as he picked up an overturned chair and righted it.

To his left, Big Mike—who, only moments before, had been ready to gut and filet him like a Mississippi catfish—was trying to put the table together again without much luck.

And there stood Cally, overseeing it all and tapping her tiny foot.

She might have Big Mike fooled, but not him, not

for a minute. She had known just how deadly serious that fight truly had been. Or at least, had started out. And she knew how to handle Big Mike.

Once she got his attention, that was. He suspected that was the hard part.

But yes sir, you had to hand it to her.

And when she glanced over at him, then quickly looked away, blushing a blush he was glad Big Mike hadn't seen, he knew something else, too.

She wanted him.

As badly as he wanted her, she wanted him just as much.

With conflicted feelings, he tried to concentrate on putting the chair back together. At least it made some sort of lopsided, splintery sense.

Nothing else in this situation did.

15

Mrs. Wallings Beaufort sat in her darkened bedroom, gazing out of the window and down the hill at the distant river, and at the lights on the boats passing silently up and down it. Moonlight glistened silver on its rolling waters, and she thought that a person would never guess how brown and choppy the water really was if they only saw it by night.

She had been sitting in this position—in her favorite armchair, upholstered in dark brocade and one of many gifts dear Wallings had bought her to help her (and himself, too) forget about their loss those many years ago. They'd gone to Europe, taken a very nice ship, and had spent a year drifting through foreign museums and feeding foreign pigeons and buying, buying, buying everything, including this chair.

And none of it had helped them forget.

None of it had eased the pain.

Once they returned, there were still the men, the men who came to the house at least one a month, it seemed: men with one hand clutching a terrified little blue-eyed boy and with the other hand held out, hoping it would be filled with the reward Wallings had promised.

Each and every time, Wallings had investigated their stories. The Beauforts' had had the Pinkertons on retainer for years. And in every case, the detectives had shaken their heads, no.

This boy was not their Teddy, nor the next, nor the next, nor the next.

She had given up. Wallings had given up more than she.

He had died.

A heart attack, the doctors said, but she knew better than they. It was his heart, all right, but it was simply broken.

Teddy had been a longed-for baby, one which had come to them late in life and very unexpectedly. She had given up on having children, accustomed herself to filling the lonely hours with arranging parties, with entertaining friends, with china painting and embroidery and being far too strict with the servants.

And then, at the advanced age of thirty-nine—when any other woman would have been looking forward to grandchildren—she had discovered that she was finally, at long last, with child.

"In a family way," Wallings always called it. He'd always been so proper, bless him.

She had spent most of her pregnancy in bed, on doctor's orders, and when the blessed event arrived— after she got over the pain of it—there was no happier, more delighted, more smitten mother in all of St. Louis.

Wallings practically busted his buttons, he was so swollen with pride.

A son.

And then the incredible had happened. A simple stroll to the park, a few moments left alone in his pram, and the baby, Teddy, was gone.

Taken.

Stolen.

Wallings had fired the nurse in a fit of rage, as if the poor girl wasn't distraught enough already.

Mrs. Beaufort—Emmy to her friends—wasn't angry with the poor nurse, and gave her a hug—and slipped twenty dollars into her pocket at the back door. No, she wasn't angry with the nurse. She was angry, livid, furious with the culprits.

She was still angry.

And more than that, she realized. She still, after all these empty years, held out hope.

She leaned forward and found the matches, then lit the lamp at her side table. Her hands looked old, she thought, freckled with age spots and large knuckled with the onset of arthritis. They were her own mother's hands, now.

Rising, she went to the mantle and pulled the bell cord. A few moments later, James rapped at her door. He was the only servant still up at this hour.

"Come in," she said, crossing her arms, thinking.

"Yes, Madam?" he said in his quiet, mannered way. "Have you decided to take a meal? Cook is still holding dinner."

"Is she?" Emmy asked, surprised. She had lost track of the time again. "Very well. I shall eat something. But tell Cook she can clean up in the morning. I don't wish to keep her from her slumbers any longer than necessary."

"Very well, Madam," James said with a small bow, and turned to leave.

"Wait," she said.

He turned about again.

"James, that woman who called this afternoon . . ." she said, trailing off.

"Yes, Madam?"

"Calista Teach, she said her name was," Emmy went on slowly, almost afraid to say the words, to open herself up for yet another in a seemingly endless string of disappointments.

She took a deep breath. "Find her. Find out about her. She lives . . ."

"Down on the docks," James finished for her. "Yes, Madam. It shall be done."

"First thing in the morning," she said.

"Very well, first thing," he replied. He paused for a moment, then added, "Shall I tell Cook to lay out your supper now?"

She nodded. "Yes, James. I shall be down in a few moments."

He left, the door closing softly behind him, and she put out a hand to steady herself on the mantel.

"Again, it starts," she whispered.

Fargo lay uneasily on the sofa. The chairs—well, most of them—had been cobbled back together, Big Mike had rigged and hammered and crossbarred the table to last through dinner, at least, and they had eaten their corned beef and cabbage like old chums.

Well, leery old chums, at least in Fargo's case.

Big Mike seemed to be in high spirits. Fargo supposed a good fight was mother's milk for him, the bastard. As for Fargo, he had some mighty sore ribs and a headache that wouldn't quit, and his head was still seeping a little blood. Cally had bandaged it for him.

But still, he thought about her. She was back there, in that dark bedroom with Big Mike. That last being the operative phrase: with Big Mike.

Goddamn him.

"And all who sail in him," Fargo whispered aloud, then smiled in spite of everything.

But just for a second.

He heard a sound, something creaking back in the hall, and stiffened. A door opened, then clicked closed. Footsteps—heavy footsteps trying to sneak— came up the hall toward the main room.

Fargo feigned sleep, but through one slitted eye he watched Big Mike Matthews creep rather ineffectually across the room, ease open the front door, and let himself out.

Now, where was that son of a bitch going? By rights, he should be moaning on a bed of pain. Or at least, soaking in a vat of liniment. Fargo wished that he, himself, was in that vat, anyhow.

Fargo was torn. On one hand, there was Cally right down the hall, all alone and probably available. On the other, there was Big Mike to follow.

It was a rough decision, but one that had to be made quickly.

Sighing, he sat up, stiffly pulled on his boots and put on his jacket. He grabbed his hat at the door, gave one lingering look down the dark hallway, then silently let himself out.

A few moments later, footsteps crept up the hall again.

Cally's footsteps.

She tiptoed out across the front room, toward the sofa, which was a scant silver outline in the darkened room.

"Mr. Drinkwater?" she whispered softly. "Larry?"

No answer.

She knelt beside the sofa, hesitated, then gently reached out for Drinkwater and found . . . nothing.

"What?" she said, and angrily felt the pillow, the blanket, then ripped them off and threw them on the floor in a heap.

Fisted hands akimbo, she growled, "Men!" and stomped back down the hall.

Fargo followed Big Mike at the distance of about a block.

This late, the streets were deserted save for the small crowds that gathered around the bars and saloons and gaming houses. Between these little islands of inebriated humanity, footsteps echoed on brick streets. The occasional low, muffled moan issued from an alley's mouth: a streetwalker at work.

More likely, her client. The way he understood it, whores didn't usually moan unless you paid them extra. Of course, that hadn't been the case in his experience, but then, you never could tell what kind of show those gals put on when they were with other men.

Big Mike went directly to the big building that was Dawber's hangout, went under the NO TRESPASSING sign, and disappeared inside. Fargo waited across the street for a decent interval, then slipped across and into the building.

He paused once he got inside and let his eyes adjust to the gloom. Thin moonlight leaked in through the broken windows of an enormous room with a high ceiling. The floor was covered in broken glass, scattered wood scraps, bits of paper, and other rubble. It obviously hadn't been used in a good, long time.

But there was a path of sorts, cleared by many footsteps, that led back to the stairs.

Above, he heard Big Mike—or at least, he assumed it was Big Mike—traveling heavy-footed up what sounded like the last flight of stairs. The boot steps were regular, high up and far away, and then they stopped.

Fargo heard a faint rap, then a door swinging on its hinges, then closing again.

Stealthily, Fargo crept up the steps. He knew that if he ran afoul of Big Mike again this night, he likely wouldn't come out on top and it wouldn't end in laughter, no matter how forced. He was too bruised from the evening's earlier festivities.

But he had to go up, to listen, to try to hear whether Toby was in that goddamn attic or not.

And just maybe hear a little of what Big Mike was up to. He suspected it wasn't any good. Not any good at all.

At last, after testing each step, he managed to get up to the third floor, down a long, narrow hall, and to a closed door. He didn't try the latch. Someone might be watching.

Instead, he crouched down and put his ear to the keyhole.

He heard something, all right. Mumbles and murmurs, the sounds of two men talking. Dawber and Big Mike. It took Fargo a second to filter out the extraneous sounds, but he was able to pick out a few words.

"Cally" came clear as a bell, then something indecipherable, then something that sounded like "bow" and "ford" and then, the magic word, "Toby."

In fact, Dawber raised his voice. He was calling the boy, Fargo realized, and in a second, he heard Toby's voice answer.

Thank God.

Then he heard Toby mutter something he couldn't make out, then Big Mike, then Dawber again. The voices weren't raised in anger. He couldn't even detect any animosity in them.

He realized that he wasn't doing anyone—himself included—any good out here.

And he sure as hell wasn't going in there.

Content that Toby was safe, at least for the moment, he started carefully back down the hall, then down the stairs. He almost made it to the second floor, too, before a board cracked under his weight.

And cracked loudly.

He heard the scramble of feet overhead, and he didn't wait to hear the door open. He just ran.

He raced down the next stairs full-out, stumbling in the dark but somehow able to keep his feet under him, always hearing the footsteps thundering behind him. There was a torrent of them, it seemed.

On the first floor, he dashed for the door and once outside, turned the opposite of the way he'd come in. He ran back down the alley, and straight into a stinking slop of human excrement.

He didn't stop.

He slipped and slid his way down that alley, to the street, then ran as hard as his bruised ribs and aching lungs would let him, back up toward town, away from Cally's place.

And when Fargo couldn't run anymore, when he was certain that Big Mike and his cohorts had likely stopped blocks behind him—panting and gasping for breath like a string of bullheads pulled onto the docks, he hoped—he slowly turned back down toward the river.

His clothes were a stinking, sewage-spattered mess. When he got down to the street that fronted the river, he crossed it before he got into the thick of the saloon district and went down to the nearest dock.

There, in the dark, he took off his trousers and washed them as best he could, then gave his boots a good scrub.

He gave his pants a wringing. They didn't stink now, except of the river, but that was bad enough. He pulled them on over clammy legs, and slowly walked back up to Cally's.

16

"Why's your britches damp, Drinkwater?" said Big Mike's voice, awakening Fargo with a start.

He opened his eyes to see the dawn sunlight creeping through the ratty curtains of the front room. Big Mike stood there, glowering at him and feeling his goddamn britches, which he'd set on a chair to dry.

Fargo sat up. He opened his mouth, but before anything had a chance to come out, Cally came down the hall.

"Aw, what you gettin' all steamed up about, Mike?" she asked, and grabbed Fargo's still damp pants out of his hands. "And you got a lot of nerve, Mike, comin' in so damned late. Or so early."

With a prettily wrinkled brow, she felt the cuffs. "Sorry, Mr. Drinkwater. Thought these would be dry by now."

Big Mike hoisted a brow, and Fargo did the same. What was she up to?

"Well, you were gone last night, Mike, and I couldn't sleep," Cally said. She folded the trousers and put them over the back of the chair again. "Drinkwater, here, was sleepin' like a log, so I couldn't exactly engage him in conversation."

"So you took his pants off'n him and dumped water on 'em," said Big Mike, with a threat in his voice.

Cally rolled her eyes. "No, you big oaf. He already had 'em off. I seen there was some mud on one'a the legs and I tried to wash it out. The damned things fell all the way into the wash basin. Sorry about that, Drinkwater."

Judiciously, she felt them again. "Well, I'll put 'em out on the back stoop. Sun's comin' up. They'll dry quick enough."

And with that, she snatched them off the chair and disappeared down the hall with them. Fargo heard the back door open and the screen bang.

Big Mike shook his head. His expression was one of wonderment mixed with disgust, and complete lack of understanding. "Women," he said.

Fargo stared after her, too, although his amazement was mixed with a great deal of gratitude—and not just a little lust.

"Yeah," he echoed. "Women."

Her heart beating so rapidly that she thought it might escape her chest, Cally spread Drinkwater's britches out over the porch rail, smoothing them. Where on earth had Drinkwater been last night?

Swimming in the river, by the faint smell still clinging to his pants.

That didn't make any sense. But neither did Drinkwater. Still, she liked him.

She liked him a great deal, actually. Oh, he was handsome, that was for certain, but she had learned long ago that handsome is as handsome does. And Drinkwater was a real nice man. He was polite, for one thing, and she was pretty certain that he'd never, not once in his life, hit a woman.

That went an awfully long way with Cally.

So she'd told Mike that she'd got Drinkwater's britches wet. Wherever Drinkwater had been, it was Drinkwater's business. Not Mike's, not hers. And she didn't want another fight like the brawl last night taking place in her front room.

Actually, she didn't want it taking place anywhere. Why, Big Mike must outweigh Drinkwater by sixty pounds, at least!

Now, that wasn't close to a fair fight.

It was a miracle that Drinkwater had been able to hold his own like he had. He was a keen scrapper, that one.

"Cally! Woman!" Big Mike hollered from inside. The lout. "Get in here and fix me somethin' to eat!"

"Hold your horses!" she hollered back.

Where had he been? It was a mystery, all right. She planned to quiz Drinkwater about it later, if and when she had the chance.

Giving a final pat to the damp trousers, she turned and went back inside.

James C. Donovan, butler to Mrs. Wallings Beaufort, sat quietly in the outer office of Detective Rawlings of the St. Louis Police Department. It wasn't a particularly clean office, or a tidy one, James thought. But then, it wasn't his business, was it?

However, that bookcase could certainly use a good tidying, for starters . . .

"Mr. Donovan?" said a voice, breaking into his thoughts.

James stood up, and stood erect. "Yes, indeed, sir," he said, eyeing the short, beleaguered-looking man peering through the partially open half-glass door. An unlit cigar stuck from his mouth, and he was chewing it thoughtlessly, like a baby in its pram chews a pacifier.

The man tipped his head. "Well, come on in. Guess you're next."

James followed him into the inner office and sat on the chair opposite the desk. The desk itself was mounded with papers and files, and on top of one mound was a haphazardly balanced placard reading, "Det. Sgt. G. G. Rawlings."

"Now," said Rawlings, leaning back in his chair. "What brings a fine fellow like you so early to the police station, sir?"

James introduced himself, giving his name and who he worked for.

"That the Beaufort of the missing baby case, several years back?" Rawlings asked.

"Indeed it is, sir."

"My goodness. Quite a deal, that. I was just new on the force when it happened. Tragic," Rawlings said with a sad shake of his head. And a wag of his cigar. "St. Louis wasn't much, either. Well, nothing like it is today."

James nodded, acknowledging the comment. "I have come, on behalf of Mrs. Beaufort, to inquire about some persons of questionable repute," he said.

"Go on," said Rawlings.

James did. He gave no real details, feeling that they were best held back, but gave the names of Calista Teach and the mysterious Dawber. He did tell Rawlings that Miss Teach had visited the house, though.

Rawlings nodded thoughtfully. "Well, I can't tell you much about this Teach woman. Name sounds familiar, but not wrapped up with Dawber's. Now, he's a horse of a different color."

What Rawlings told James was very interesting indeed, and James cringed at the thought of having to repeat it to Mrs. Beaufort. Suffice it to say that Dawber was a singularly unpleasant man, engaged in an extremely unpleasant business.

It seemed to James that, oddly enough, it might be possible that this Dawber did have some knowledge of young Master Teddy. Not likely, but possible. Whatever Dawber was involved with, however, would be on the shady side. Of this, James was certain.

"Why?" asked Rawlings.

"Why what, sir?"

"Why you wanna know? I just realized I been talkin' just to hear my lips flap," Rawlings said, smiling around his still-unlit cigar. His eyes were slitted with keen intelligence, though, if James was any judge.

James stood up. "Thank you, Detective Rawlings."

"Detective *Sergeant* Rawlings," Rawlings corrected him.

"Yes," said James with a small bow of his head. "Detective Sergeant. I'm terribly sorry. Thank you so much for your time, sir. We shall be in touch if we need you."

"But—"

"Again," said James, this time with a fuller bow in the doorway, "our thanks and humble gratitude. Good day, then."

And he slipped through the door, hurried down the stairs, and was out of the station and into his waiting buggy. Hopefully, before Rawlings had a chance to think twice about his abrupt departure.

Mrs. Beaufort was very keen on keeping her business to herself.

And James was just as keen on keeping the status quo.

On this morning, Toby had been held in the attic once again, while Nimble Jack, Rance the redheaded cook, his friend Toledo, and all the other boys went out to see what could be had by a nimble hand, a quick eye, and a glib tongue.

"Just you wait," Toledo had confided before he slid out the door and into the wide, waiting world, "you're gonna be rich as Croesus. Or Midas. Or one'a them fellers."

Toby sat on the edge of a crate, elbows on his knees, waiting for Dawber, who was busy inside his partially walled room. *Clink, clank, thud.* Whatever he was doing in there, it was noisy.

And probably no good, either, thought Toby.

In these short days, he had developed a healthy disrespect for Dawber. Even in the orphanage, he'd never met anybody so, well, slimy. That was the only word he could think of to describe the way Dawber made him feel. It boggled him that none of the other boys shared his sense of Dawber. Hell, they seemed to love and admire him!

Well, maybe they did, maybe not. Dawber's loft and Dawber's sideways militancy didn't exactly foster coming forward with the unvarnished truth about much of anything.

Not that Toby was the best at truth telling, but Dawber's little amoral army of thieves made him feel like a choir boy.

And that Mike fellow gave him the shivers, too. He'd been here all last night, talking with Dawber. Well, except for the time when they broke it off because Big Mike heard somebody downstairs. Or thought he did.

Toby sure wouldn't want to have Big Mike Matthews after *him*.

But he'd come back empty-handed, and he and Dawber had talked the night away.

Toby couldn't make out much of what they were saying, and frankly, he'd fallen asleep right after Big Mike's return. He couldn't help but think they were up to something rotten, though, especially since Mike didn't bring Cally with him.

Toledo had told him that Mike always brought Cally, save when he and Dawber were planning something really big. And Toby couldn't help but think that he was supposed to play some part in it. He'd picked out his name from the hum of their conversation once or twice, and it had scared him.

As much as he admired Fargo, he hadn't counted on being locked in an attic with no windows and forced to do some big, awful thing that he'd probably get caught for. And either get himself hanged or spend the rest of his life in jail.

He shuddered.

And all for two hundred and fifty dollars and the pleasure of knowing Skye Fargo, king of the penny dreadfuls.

He didn't even know if Fargo was out there. Why, he could have lit out for Omaha or Santa Fe or somewhere the minute he saw Toby hitch that ride!

But then, why would he have forked over the ten dollars? Why would he have gone to all the trouble to feed Toby and talk to him and make up that story about his old friend Armstrong and a missing ruby ring?

Why hadn't Fargo simply hauled him over to the sheriff's office when Fargo found him trying to make off with the Ovaro?

It made no sense, no sense at all.

More bumps and thuds issued from behind Dawber's makeshift wall, and Toby sighed.

But then, he got to thinking.

What if that person Big Mike had chased away last night was Fargo, in the flesh? What if he was really out there, and had traced Toby to this very address? What if Fargo was worried about him?

Toby shook his head and gave a little snort.

Not hardly likely. Nobody in his whole life had ever worried about him. Why should Fargo be any different?

Toby was dreaming again. Toby, the daydreamer, just like Old Man Stevens, back at the orphanage, used to call him.

He sank his head down on propped hands, and waited for Dawber.

17

There, thought Dawber, and rubbed his hands together. *All my precious little treasures back in their nooks and crannies once again.*

He sat down on the edge of his mattress and ran a soiled and wrinkled handkerchief over his brow. All was right with the world again.

Now, to Toby.

He rose and found his pair of scissors, then found the honing strap and gave the blades a few swipes. He held them up in the air. *Snip, snip.*

They'd do.

"Toby, my dear?" he called as he walked out into the main space.

The boy was right where he'd left him, waiting patiently. Dawber smiled.

"Yes sir," said Toby, and stood up.

So polite, this dear one. They probably strapped and beat and willow-switched it into them at the orphanages. Whatever the method, they'd done a good job. At first, he hadn't been happy about the "sirs" and the "pleases," but then, once he'd thought about it, it made him very happy indeed.

The Beaufort boy would be polite, wouldn't he?

He certainly would, just by the fact that he was a Beaufort, if nothing else.

Breeding will tell, you know, he thought to himself.

Not that he believed a word of it.

He held the scissors out and worked the blades. "Let's get to that mop of yours, my dear," he said, smiling.

Toby looked a tad nervous, but he sat down again and tucked his collar under.

Ah, so well-trained, this boy is.

Dawber turned up the lantern and began to cut a boy out of this hairy little beast.

Fifteen years ago, he had been in on the plot to kidnap the Beaufort boy and hold him for ransom. Beaufort was from New York, where Dawber had once worked the town, and there was bad blood between the two.

That is, Dawber held something against Beaufort. Dawber doubted whether Beaufort even knew Dawber's name. Dawber had come across the seas from England with a wife in tow, a pretty young wife called Maisie.

He had been a different man, then.

Well, a sort of different man. He wasn't above using the law for his own advantage, and ignoring it when it pleased him. Although his family had something against his modus operandi—and they had, for they'd cast him out and sent him packing once the courts were through with him—his dearest, darling Maisie had no such lofty compunctions.

Dawber had rigged a stock fraud. Things were going very well, too. Maisie was with child, their first, and he planned to make some real money from this deal.

Except that Beaufort had been the one to see through the plot and bring it down, the man who'd reduced Dawber to living in a hovel instead of a lovely brick and mortar town house, the stinking bastard who'd had the police hounding him and putting not a few of his friends in jail.

And in Dawber's mind, Beaufort was also the man who'd killed his Maisie and their unborn child, killed them with nothing but shame and poverty in that dark, cold winter of his ruin.

And so, years later, when Fanny Salter came to him with a plot to kidnap a boy from St. Louis, a boy with the surname of Beaufort, he had been all ears. Dawber himself had snatched the baby from his perambulator, handed him off to Fanny at the docks, and caught the first stage for Chicago.

But then, Fanny had disappeared, and the boy with her. He followed the newspaper stories religiously, but could find no mention of a ransom!

He was livid at first, then just angry, and eventually, simply bitter. Fanny had done him wrong, which he began to believe was what you should expect from a Chicago whore and confidence artist.

He had no idea what Fanny wanted that kid for, but it obviously wasn't the money. There was nothing in the papers about a ransom note.

And then he heard a rumor that Fanny's body had washed up down river from St. Louis, not long after he'd handed her the baby at the docks.

Bloody bitch, he'd thought at the time, *getting herself killed when she had a kid worth thousands. Just like her.*

And so he stopped hating Fanny quite so much— after all, she was dead and couldn't suffer from it— and forgot about the whole thing. If Fanny had gone over the rail, it was fairly certain that the youngster had gone with her and had been washed down river.

Perhaps out to sea.

Of course, maybe it hadn't lasted that long. Babies had such soft flesh, easily nibbled and eaten by river fish and turtles, he'd thought. Young Teddy had likely made a tender morsel for the crawfish and eels.

He got a little pleasure from that, at least.

But now, after all these years, he was going to get his money from Wallings Beaufort. Or rather, Beaufort's widow.

"All things come to those who wait," he muttered, smiling.

Toby said, "What's that?"

"Nothing, my dear," Dawber said, snipping away, never missing a beat. "Nothing at all."

Life was about to be very sweet.

Big Mike had stomped out of the house five minutes ago, leaving Fargo—still wrapped in a sheet—and Cally alone.

Cally had gone to the stove, ostensibly to fry some more bacon and eggs for him and for herself, but more probably, Fargo decided, to give her an excuse to avoid talking to him. The sexual tension in the room was as thick as paste.

At last, he couldn't stand it any longer. He broke the silence, and asked, "Why, Cally?"

It was enough. She knew. She said, "Because I didn't want another fight." She was still turned away from him.

Tripping a little over his sheet, he went to the kitchen where she was lifting eggs, done over easy, from a skillet onto two plates. He touched her shoulder and she turned.

"Cally," he began.

"Don't say it," she interrupted. "Don't be grateful. It's just self-preservation."

"Stop," he said. "You know what I was going to say, and it didn't have anything to do with Mike."

"Everything has to do with Mike," she said, and set the skillet, the half-fried bacon still bubbling, off the burner.

"Not everything."

She looked down at the floor. "No," she said softly. "I guess it doesn't."

"He coming back soon?"

"No," she said, looking up again. She had the most beautiful eyes. "He's gone down to the Little Cougar to meet the boys. He'll likely have a few beers, laugh too much, brag too much, then fall asleep." She shrugged. "At least, that's what he usually does after he's out all night."

Fargo touched her face. "Cally, do you want out of this? This whole thing?"

"Don't be silly. There's no 'out' for me. This is it."

Fargo put his hands on her shoulders. "There's always a door, Cally."

She whispered, "No, not for me," and a tear trickled slowly down one cheek.

Fargo wrapped her in his arms, and she clung to him, soundlessly weeping.

"Shh," he breathed into her hair, then inhaled its scent. It smelled of lemons. "Shh, it's all right, baby."

"No," he heard her mumble into his shoulder. "No. It'll never be all right again, Drinkwater."

"It can be, Cally," he whispered. "Leave it to me. I can fix it. I can fix anything. I can take you to another place, another town. You could start over, all brand new and shiny."

"You can't fix this," she said, untucking her head and gazing up into his eyes. "Nobody can."

And then her gaze seemed to go deeper, right inside him.

Rising on her tiptoes, she kissed him gently, almost tentatively at first, then hard and deep. Hungrily. And Fargo was certain that she had wanted this as much as he had—that she, too, had been longing for it, just waiting for an overt sign.

He swept her into his arms and carried her to the sofa, never breaking the kiss, and he settled her down on the pillows.

Huskily, she whispered, "Yes, Drinkwater . . ."

He ripped at her clothes, tearing them away, and she tore at his shirt. His sheet dropped away, and he mounted her.

At first, he wanted her so much that he was nearly brutal, but he was soon in control. His moves went from hard and fast to sensuous and slow.

She moved beneath him, twisting, gyrating, rising to meet his every thrust. And she made sounds, wonderful sounds. She whispered, "My God" or "Yes, yes!" or just mewled something indecipherable.

It was all coal to his furnace, fed the flames of his lust for her higher and higher.

She wrapped her legs about him, hugged him hard. Her head was craned back and her eyes were closed.

Fargo became as lost in his own sensations as she

117

was in hers. He rode her like a tick stuck fast to a hound, penetrating, never letting go, never wanting to. And then he began to move faster again, to feel the tickle in his loins grow to a flame, then a bonfire that he was powerless to stop.

As he roared to fruition, she, too, came with a loud, shivering cry. She shuddered uncontrollably beneath him as he made his final thrusts and felt the explosion rocket throughout him, race through his veins and every nerve in his body.

He clung to her, and she to him, both panting, both slick with sweat. And the first thing Fargo thought, when he opened his eyes and propped himself up and looked down at her, was that he hadn't realized what absolutely beautiful breasts she had.

How beautiful she was all over, really. What a waste of a precious flower, to plant her here in a field of onions.

He slid from within her, but she still held him close. "Drinkwater," she murmured, her eyes still half-slitted. She smiled contentedly. "Or should I call you Larry?"

He made a quick decision.

He said, "You should call me Fargo."

She opened her eyes the rest of the way. "Fargo? Why Fargo?"

He sat up and perched on the edge of the sofa. "Because that's my real name, Cally. I didn't like fooling you."

Surprised but curious, she looked at him quizzically. "Then why pick Drinkwater? Why not Smith or Green or Foster?"

He shrugged. "First one that came to mind, actually."

She pulled herself up on her elbows, and her ripe breasts took on an even rounder form with the shift. "All right. But Fargo?"

He shrugged his shoulders and smiled. "Can't help it. Was born with it."

"But that's like that man in the books the kids read. You know, that cocksure son of a . . ." Her eyes narrowed. She said, "No."

"Yup," Fargo admitted, although he hated to. He was embarrassed.

Cally let out a hoot. "You're joshing! That Fargo? *The* Fargo?"

"Can we move onto something else?" Fargo said, grinning sheepishly. He'd had no idea this would affect her this way.

"Listen," she said, sitting all the way up and leaning closer, "you can't tell Mike about this. Never. You got that?"

He had no intention of telling Big Mike his real name, and just as little interest in telling him that he'd just slept with Cally.

But he said, "Which?"

Cally made a face. "About everything! He'd kill you, sure as shootin'." And then she seemed to be talking to herself. "I just slept with *the* Skye Fargo! Holy Moses!"

Fargo frowned.

Cally burst out laughing. "I'm teasin' you, Drinkwater," she said, once she got herself under control. "You're not Fargo, and I'm no fool. Everybody knows Skye Fargo always wears buckskins, like the Indians do, and rides that big paint stallion. And besides, he's just made-up, anyhow!"

She laughed again, then said, "What do you take me for, anyway?"

Fargo's frown had quickly turned into a grin. If she didn't believe him, well, she didn't believe him. At least she couldn't come back later and say that he'd fed her a complete pack of lies.

He winked at her and answered by saying, "Nobody's fool, Cally."

"You're sure somethin' to reckon with, Drinkwater," she said, more softly.

He kissed her again.

18

"I see," said Emmy Beaufort. "Very well. Thank you, James."

He bowed slightly and left her and she sat down on the couch to think over what he'd said. He hadn't really made any comment—butlers rarely did, after all—but while he was telling her about this Mr. Dawber, a slight nuance of distaste had come into his voice.

Actually, if it hadn't, she would have been quite surprised. She had never laid an eye on Dawber, never even heard of him before yesterday, but she'd like to wring his neck just on general principle.

No wonder James felt much the same way. Or so she suspected.

She sat at the window for at least a half hour, engrossed in thought, before she stood up and went to the fireplace. She put her hand on the bellpull and gave it a little tug. A few moments later, James rapped at the door.

"I have come to a decision, James," she said.

"Yes, Madam?"

"I should like you to take the buggy out again. I want you to find our Miss Teach and bring her here, if you can."

"Very good," he said. "When would you wish me to depart, Madam?"

"What time is it now?"

He slipped a gloved hand into his vest pocket and extracted a pocket watch. "Precisely a quarter to eleven," he said, snapping it closed with an efficient sounding *click*. James was always so proper, so exact, God bless him. He put her a little in mind of her late husband.

Except that Wallings had been, well, Wallings. And James was only an English butler.

Emmy said, "Then after luncheon would be soon enough, James. That's all."

She thought that the smallest hint of a smile spread across his usually stoic face.

"Yes indeed, Madam," he replied with a nod. "Yes indeed. I should be most delighted."

When Fargo wandered up to the Little Cougar, Big Mike was, indeed, sound asleep and sawing logs at a corner table.

Cally had gone to take her friend, Grace Cooper, a basket and had promised to meet Fargo—and Mike—at the bar at around noon, so as not to raise Big Mike's suspicions.

Fargo figured he had about an hour before she showed up.

He stood in the doorway a moment, juggling his options, and came up with exactly nothing. That he could accomplish in an hour, that is.

So he sidled up to the bar. "Beer," he said to the barkeep.

As he stood there, looking out the window, a young lad walked by, a boy dressed in the next thing to rags, who wandered along the sidewalk with what seemed no aim whatsoever.

Fargo glanced at him for a moment, then was distracted by the delivery of his beer.

When he looked back, the boy had disappeared into the crowd.

"Very good, my dear," Dawber said, standing back to admire his work.

Toby felt as if he'd just been scalped, and felt his head for signs of blood.

But Dawber rather uncharacteristically laughed and said, "I'll fetch you a mirror, Toby. You're not bleeding, I promise you."

Toby wasn't so sure until he looked at himself in the badly silvered hand mirror. He twisted and turned by the light of several oil lamps, but all he saw was a rather nice haircut. No open wounds to speak of.

He handed the mirror back. "Looks good," he admitted.

Dawber set the mirror down on a crate. His hands went to his hips and he studied Toby up and down.

"Clothes," he said at last. "Now we need some new clothing. Nothing fancy, you mind. I won't make you dress in that suit." He flung a hand toward the trunk that the ruffle and blue velvet had come from, and Toby heaved a small sigh of relief. "Just something . . . tidier."

And then he did something that Toby had wished for, but hadn't dared to hang his hopes on. Dawber strode across the expanse of attic, opened the door, and gestured at him.

"Well?" he said, beckoning. "Come along, lad. What are you waiting for?"

"Nothin'!" cried Toby happily, and slipped past Dawber to the hall, and the staircase beyond.

Dawber carried on quite the conversation as they walked down the streets, headed for the riverfront. It was a rather one-sided conversation, but Toby didn't mind. He was too busy breathing in what passed for fresh air around these parts, and enjoying the sunshine. He'd surely missed the sun.

He caught a little of what Dawber was saying, though. It was something about not looking *too* spit and polish. After all, Dawber said, Toby had been in an orphanage, then out on his own. He shouldn't look too good, but then, he shouldn't look so bad that she wouldn't embrace him, either.

Toby decided that Mrs. Beaufort must be a wooden-headed old lady if she'd accept a person—or not—as her very own son based on the threads he wore, but he didn't say anything.

Now, he had no hopes whatsoever that he was going to change his name to Beaufort. The possibility, quite frankly, hadn't really crossed his mind. He just wanted to find Fargo. He wanted to explain that he couldn't find the damned ring, and that if Fargo didn't mind, he'd just as soon wander off someplace and Fargo could forget about the two-fifty.

That's what he'd decided, anyhow. Ten dollars wasn't enough pay for being locked in an attic and having to piss and shit out a window, especially when you hadn't known, right up to this very minute, that you were ever going to see the sky again, or see a bird, or feel the wind on your face.

No, ten bucks wasn't enough, but he'd be damned if he was going to hang around to snag the two-fifty. It was impossible, anyway. He'd have to be two people to pull it off!

He could have really used a chum up in the attic. A good chum, like Bass Owen had been back at the orphanage. Boy, they'd have found and lifted that ring in slap time, and been in Kansas City by now, two hundred and fifty dollars the richer!

He smiled, thinking about what ol' Bass Owen would have done for half of two-fifty—which seemed a vast windfall—and how excited he would have been at the prospect of getting his hands on it.

"Anticipating your good fortune, my boy?" Dawber asked, bringing Toby back to earth.

"I guess so, sir," Toby replied.

When in doubt, always be polite. That was Toby's motto.

They stopped in front of a men's clothing store. It was tiny with soot and dirt-smeared windows, and showed not even the faintest signs of prosperity, but Dawber led him through the door.

A little bell jingled, and Dawber called out, "Choffey!"

A bald head peered around a wooden case full of paper-wrapped shirts (or so said the sign), and then it blossomed into a smile. "Why, Mr. Dawber! How nice to see you!"

The bald head—upon a short and portly body—emerged into the aisle, and came toward them. The two men shook hands, and Dawber said, "Toby, meet Mr. Archibald Choffey. Today, he will invent you. Clothes make the man, you know."

"How you doin', sir?" Toby said, his gaze curiously searching every nook and cranny of the shop.

It didn't look like Mr. Choffey had a cleaning woman come in. Ever.

In fact, when Choffey chose a shirt for him, still in its packaging, he blew the dust from it in a large cloud that left Toby coughing.

"Sickly, is he?" Choffey asked Dawber.

Dawber said, "Oh, the lad will be right as rain. Won't you, boy?"

"Yes sir, I will," replied Toby, staring past Dawber's shoulder and up at a rather elaborate spider's web, complete with a large, spinning spider. He gulped and added, "I reckon."

At long last, after a great deal of trying on this or that and measuring and chin rubbing and *hmmm*ing, they completed their business with Mr. Choffey.

"One more stop," said Dawber, after they walked out on the street again. Toby was loaded with boxes full of clothes he didn't much like, but which Dawber and Choffey had agreed were perfect.

They had a lopsided idea of perfection, if you asked Toby. And he'd found out that Mr. Choffey was color blind, which Toby didn't expect helped too much in Choffey's line of work.

They proceeded up the way to another store, into which Dawber disappeared, saying, "Don't move a muscle, my dear."

And Toby didn't. For a minute, at least.

But then he saw something that, at first, he thought

was a mirage. He blinked, moved his head back behind the pile of boxes in his arms, then looked again.

He didn't even dare smile. He just shifted the boxes a tad and said, in a voice too small to carry far, "B-Bass? Bass Owen?"

When there was no response—and he realized that he couldn't be heard by anybody farther away than a foot, he raised his voice, this time shouting.

"Bass! Is that you, Bass Owen?"

The boy he'd seen down the street, the boy he'd thought was a mirage, turned toward him, stared, then broke out in a huge grin.

"Toby? Toby Jones?" he shouted. "As I live and breathe!"

Bass broke into a run and Toby shot toward him, dropping his boxes where he stood. The two boys met and hugged, then thought better of it and slapped each other's back repeatedly.

Neither of them, it seemed could stop grinning.

"I thought you was dead or somethin'!" Bass exclaimed gleefully. "Goddamn it, if you ain't a sight for these sore eyes! You livin' here? You got a job? A place to stay?"

A shout from the place from which Toby had come got both of their attentions.

"*Toby!*" shouted Dawber, pointing to the packages carelessly dropped on the street. He looked miles past angry, and Toby was suddenly mortally afraid.

"What," roared Dawber, "do you mean by this!?"

19

James, dressed in shabbier than usual clothing, stepped down from the buggy several blocks away from the dock area. His mode of dress was mildly offensive to his sense of propriety, but he told himself that it was a necessary evil.

"Go on," he said to his driver. "I shall hire a cab home."

Max, Mrs. Beaufort's driver of long-standing, sat slumped on the driver's seat, the reins hanging loose in his aged-spotted hands.

"You sure, James?" Max asked in his scratchy voice. "This ain't a usual part of town for a gent like you. Why, down there, it's like back in the fur trader days. It's wild I tell you! Only more crowded, I reckon, and each one'a them waterfront toughs has got him a blade or worse. I wouldn't go down there without a weapon if I was you. Hellfire!" he exclaimed in one final burst of oratory energy. "I wouldn't go down there without an army!"

James, mildly amused but still more than a little leery, said, "Thank you for the warning, but I shall be all right. Go on your way now, Max."

"Iffen you say so," Max said with a shrug of his thin shoulders. "But just you remember. If'n you gets yourself sliced up or killed, I told you so!"

Max clucked to the horses, Daisy and Moses, and they moved slowly off down the street.

Best get on with it, old chum, James thought. He set

126

out toward the docks, but he reached into his pocket and touched the revolver he'd secreted there.

Max might be an old woman about some things, but he was at least partially correct about this part of town. James would be ready.

He hoped.

Fargo had thought better of it and leaving Big Mike, still sound asleep at the back table, took a quick run to his hotel to get rid of all but a hundred dollars of his money, then to the livery to check on the Ovaro.

He was short on time, so he didn't give his horse more than a cursory going over and a couple of scratches on the neck.

"Looks like they're takin' good care of you, boy," he said softly. "Won't be much longer before we're back on the trail again."

The horse whickered and nudged Fargo with his nose.

He gave the stallion a final pat, and as he left the stable, he muttered, "If the Good Lord's willing, that is."

It was time for him to be meeting Cally and Big Mike, and as he hurried back toward the waterfront, he hoped that Mike would sleep right through lunch, too. Things would sure be easier.

But when he walked back into the Little Cougar, Mike was sitting up, wide awake, and full of piss and vinegar. "Hey, Drinkwater!" he shouted, and Fargo had no choice but to answer him with a forced smile and a wave.

He pulled up a chair at Big Mike's table, ordered something to eat and the obligatory beer, and Mike did the same.

Fargo was hungrier than he'd suspected, and even the stingy, stringy roast beef sandwiches they served at the Little Cougar tasted good to him. But he was a little worried. He'd been watching out the window, and hadn't caught a glimpse of Cally yet.

"Thought Cally was gonna meet us here," he said, chewing.

Big Mike hoisted a brow. "She tell you that?"

Fargo nodded.

"Well, don't count on nothin' Cally says," Mike announced. "She's always gettin' caught up in her goddamn charity work, like that old woman she's keepin' alive by the skin of her teeth."

Mike craned his shaggy head to see the wall clock. "She'd best get her fat ass down here pretty soon, though. Time she was clockin' in and on the job, the lazy snippet."

Those were fighting words to Fargo, but he didn't dare let Big Mike get under his skin right now. Everything was hanging in the balance, and he did mean *everything*.

"You were gone ~~all~~ last night, like Cally said?" he asked, trying to sound casual.

Mike nodded, his attention elsewhere.

"Out playin' poker?"

"What?" Mike asked. "Naw, I don't play cards. That's for suckers. Just had some business, that's all. Hey, you!" he shouted suddenly—and angrily—toward the bar. "Hey, dog balls for brains! Can I get a couple more beers over here?"

The bartender glared back at him, but drew the beers and delivered them without comment.

Must be nice to be so loved and admired, Fargo thought dryly.

It was obvious that almost every man in the place would have gladly seen Big Mike Matthews floating facedown in the river.

And equally obvious that not one among them was about to take the first step toward that goal. No, they were going to keep on smiling and scraping and pretending until Big Mike either moved along or died.

And Fargo knew which one he preferred. He imagined that if he took a vote, he could get an overwhelming majority of *Aye*s.

Cally still hadn't appeared, and Fargo was growing antsy. When she hadn't made an appearance by one o'clock, he stood up and excused himself.

"Leavin' so soon?" Big Mike asked. If he was worried in the least about Cally's tardiness, he certainly didn't show it.

"Got business," Fargo said amiably. "You're not the only man on the river with things to do and people to see, Mike."

"Someday you're gonna have to tell me what you do all day, Drinkwater," Big Mike said.

" 'Bout the same time you tell me your business," Fargo quipped.

Big Mike took it well, which was what Fargo was hoping for. He just wanted to get out of here and scare up Cally. Or scare up Toby.

Whichever came first.

"Let go of me!" Cally demanded, batting at the restraining arm which had just pulled her into an alley. "I said, leave me go!"

"There, there, Miss Teach," said a slightly familiar voice, and she turned and looked up at a familiar, but unplaced face.

"Who are you?" she demanded, shaking herself free. The man didn't fight her, just backed off a foot or two and let go.

"If you will remember, Miss Teach, I am James," he said. "Mrs. Wallings Beaufort's butler."

"Oh, yeah," she said softly. "The clothes are different, but I remember the face now. What you doin' down in this part of town? She didn't send you for me, did she?" she asked, hardly daring to hope.

"As a matter of fact, yes," James intoned.

"She believes my story then," said Cally, and her nerves, on the edge of hysteria since yesterday, at last relaxed.

Well, her nerves had relaxed this morning with Drinkwater, but that didn't mean that Big Mike and Dawber wouldn't kill her. It just meant that she'd managed to forget about her dilemma for a little while in Drinkwater's arms.

And what arms they were!

"No," James was saying. "I don't believe that is the

case. However, she would like to see you again. Today, if at all possible."

Cally cocked her head. Things were going more swimmingly that she'd ever imagined. She smiled, and asked, "When?"

"Right now, if you would, Miss," the ill-dressed butler said. She'd never seen anyone look more uncomfortable in her whole life.

"Sure," she said, stepping from the alley's mouth and heading up the hill, away from the river and toward town, proper. "That'd be dandy."

James scrambled to walk on her right, on the side nearest the road, and offered his arm.

"You're a real gent, ain't you, James?" she asked, grinning.

"I shall hail us a cab when I see one," he said, by way of an answer.

Cally smiled and walked on.

After searching the side streets for Cally and coming up empty, Fargo had headed down toward Dawber's place. It was a slim chance, but he thought he might catch a glimpse of Toby, and if he was lucky, get to talk to him briefly. Find out how things were going.

And if they were going badly, yank the kid the hell out of there. Fargo would buy Armstrong a goddamn glass ring to replace his lost one, and he'd do it out of his own pocket, too.

But when he was only halfway there, still in the streets that were doing some commerce, he stopped stock still.

There, in the middle of the street, stood Dawber. And Toby, newly shorn.

And some kid he couldn't place.

And they were having some kind of row, all right. Fargo couldn't tell what they were talking about, but by the look on Dawber's face, he was none too happy about something. Probably what the boys had done, because he shook his finger first in Toby's face, then the other boy's, then Toby's again.

Fargo took a deep breath, prayed that Toby had half the sense he was born with, and then he forced a big grin onto his face. He walked forward, waving his hand in a greeting, and called, "Hello, Dawber! Is that you, old chum?"

Dawber, one hand lifted and just about to strike Toby, paused. He dropped his arm and made some semblance of a smile.

"Yes," he called. "Hello, Drinkwater."

Fargo's legs moved faster, and soon he had joined the little group. "How are you doing, Dawber?" he asked. "And might I ask who your friends are?"

Lord bless him, Toby stepped right up, stuck out his hand, and said, "Toby Jones, sir. Real pleased to meetcha, Mr. . . . Drinkwater, was it?"

"Yup, that's me," Fargo enthused. "Larry Drinkwater, from up to Des Moines."

The other boy stuck out his hand, which was somewhat grimier than Toby's, and said, "Bass, Mr. Drinkwater. Bass Owen."

"I was just tellin' Mr. Dawber, here," Toby said. "Bass and me are old friends from back at the orphanage. Ain't seen each other in years, and we just run into each other, right here in the danged street. It's like a miracle or something."

"Like a miracle!" echoed Bass.

"Enough!" Dawber practically shouted, and then he got control of himself once more. Fargo could tell he was right on the edge.

"Sorry, sir," said Toby. "Me and Bass, we'll pick up those boxes right away."

And in the instant before Toby turned away, he signaled Fargo to keep Dawber busy for a few seconds.

At least, that's what Fargo thought he was signaling.

So he said, "You live around this part of town, Mr. Dawber?"

"No," came the reply. Dawber's voice was irritated, curt, and on the verge of rude.

Too bad, thought Fargo. "You got a business

131

around here someplace?" he asked. "Like to stop in and see it sometime."

"Once again, Mr. Drinkwater, no," Dawber snapped. "Where's Big Mike?"

Fargo tipped his head. "Oh, he's likely still at the Little Cougar. That's where I left him, anyhow. Likes his beer, that one. Course," he added with a wink, "I'm fond of it myself."

"I shall be seeing you, Mr. Drinkwater," Dawber said abruptly, and turned on his heel.

"Sure," Fargo called after him. "Be seeing you, Dawber!"

He watched as Dawber and Toby, laden with the packages he and his friend Bass had picked up, went up the street toward Dawber's little den of iniquity. Fargo frowned. He didn't even notice Bass's approach.

"Mr. Drinkwater?"

Startled, Fargo turned. "Oh. Yes, Bass?"

"Mr. Drinkwater, I'm to tell you somethin'. I'm to say that Toby can't find the you-know-what, whatever that is, and that Dawber's gonna sell him to . . . damn! Can't remember the name!"

"Think, boy!" Fargo almost shouted. That Toby couldn't find the ring was almost immaterial at this point.

"It's somethin' long and real different. Walleye, maybe? Or Wallace. Mrs. Wallace Beaufort? He said they were going to palm him off or somethin'." He paused, then added, "Toby said you'd give me a buck."

What had he heard last night? Something that sounded like bow ford. Beaufort, of course! Not Walleye, or even Wallace, but . . . Wallings! The Wallings Beaufort case?

Good God!

Oh, he remembered that one, all right. It had been long ago and he hadn't been much more than a teenager himself, but he remembered it.

Suddenly, he said, "Bass, I can do a whole lot better than a dollar."

Bass cocked his head. His eyes narrowed with the

look of a boy who's been cheated more than a few times by fast talkers. "What do you mean?"

"If you do what I say—and you help Toby out of a tight spot—I'll give you twenty bucks." Fargo dug into his pocket, glancing quickly down the street to make sure that Dawber was out of sight. He was.

"Here," he said, handing over three shiny silver cartwheels. "Take this on account."

"Gee," Bass said, bug-eyed and staring at the money as if it were some sort of magic charm. Then he looked up, his brows knitted. "Toby's in Dutch? Who with? What'd he do?"

At that moment, Fargo realized that the boys looked enough alike—or would, once you got them both cleaned up—to be brothers. Which of course, was why he'd noticed him from the Little Cougar window.

However, he brushed the thought aside. There were more important things to deal with.

"He didn't do anything," he said. "And I'll explain it all later, all right? In the meantime, I want you to go up to the Shea Hotel. I've got a room there, but it's under a different name: Fargo." He reached into his pocket and pulled out his room key.

"Fargo, right," the boy repeated.

"Take this," he said, pressing it into Bass's hand. "If anybody gives you any grief, just say you're my nephew."

He glanced after Dawber again, but the street was clear. He said, "Lock yourself in the room, and don't talk to anybody, all right? I'll be there to fill you in on the situation before dark."

"Honest to gosh? A real hotel room?" Bass said, and Fargo wondered if he'd listened past that part.

But his misgivings were shortly overcome, because Bass seemed to recover himself, and said, "The Shea. Right."

"You know where it is?"

Bass nodded.

"All right," Fargo said. "Scoot."

20

"How do you do, Miss Teach," said Mrs. Beaufort. "Have a seat, please."

Cally, who had been pacing nervously ever since James told her to wait in the library, perched on the edge of a chair and waited expectantly.

Mrs. Beaufort took the chair opposite. "Normally," she began, "I would ask James to serve tea. More civilized, you know."

Cally nodded. She was acutely aware of her "working" dress, and ashamed of it. This part of town was not the place for it.

No place was, she suddenly realized.

"I want you to tell me your story again, dear," said Mrs. Beaufort. "I'm sure there are parts I didn't allow you to tell me. I was rude and curt with you, and for that I apologize. I have since come into information that leads me to believe that I should hear you out."

"Yes, ma'am," Cally said. "Where do you want me to start?"

"With this Mr. Dawber, I should imagine."

"Sure thing," Cally said, relaxing a little. She leaned forward. "See, it's like this . . ."

Cally still hadn't turned up or checked in with him, and Big Mike was past annoyed. This wasn't like her. Even if she turned a noontime trick, she'd always come up to the Little Cougar, if for nothing more than to let him know she was still alive.

And also, pay him his cut.

But no, the bitch hadn't shown her face, and it was past one. This was really pissing him off, and once he caught up with the little trollop, he'd punch her to Kingdom Come.

He walked up and down the streets, asking folks he knew if they'd seen her, acting like it was just casual, you know? "Seen Cally?" he'd ask.

When they'd shake their heads no, and ask "Why? What's wrong?" he'd make up something.

"Aw, she left her pocketbook down at the café," he'd say.

Or, "Got to tell her somethin', that's all."

That was vague enough.

He didn't want anyone to know that he'd actually lost her. That wouldn't do his reputation any good, now would it?

At last, after he'd been looking almost an hour, he ran into Skinny Phelps, one of the characters around the dock's fringes. Skinny worked for Dodge O'Reilly, who ran the local betting pools.

"Hey Skinny!" he roared, and poor little Skinny froze in his tracks.

"W-what?" Skinny asked.

He always was awful rabbity-like, Big Mike thought. Course, that probably came from his having been walloped by Big Mike once upon a time. It was a case of mistaken identity, could have happened to anybody, and Big Mike had apologized and bought him a drink, to boot.

But Skinny was still as jumpy as a frog on a stove lid around Mike.

For the thousandth time, Big Mike said, "You seen Cally today? Gotta tell her somethin'."

"N-not since a little past noon," Skinny replied, inching away.

Well this was better news than Mike had come up

with so far. He said, "Hold on there, Skinny. Where-abouts you see her?"

Skinny's shaking thumb poked back over his shoulder. "Thataway," he said. "She was walkin' up toward town with some feller."

Mike frowned. "Some feller? You ever see him before?"

Skinny shook his head. "Nope, never. Can I go now? Dodge is waitin' for me up at—"

"What'd he look like, this feller?" Big Mike growled. He'd better be a business client, that was all he had to say.

"N-not a river man," Skinny said, jumpier than ever. "Dressed too fancy. But not *too* fancy, if you know what I mean."

"No."

"I-I mean, that is, I mean that he didn't look like he was from around here," Skinny stammered. "Looked to me like he was tryin' to dress the part, but didn't quite pull it off, y'know?"

Big Mike's hand reached out and curled around Skinny's arm, which didn't do much for Skinny's confidence.

"Show me," Big Mike said. "Show me where you seen 'em."

"But Dodge is waitin'!" Skinny gasped in a futile plea.

"Don't worry about Dodge. I'll take care'a him," Big Mike said. "Now, let's move it. Skinny? You listenin' to me?"

"Y-yeah, yeah, B-Big Mike, I'm listenin'," peeped Skinny. "T-this way."

Toby had to jog trot to keep up with Dawber. It wasn't easy, what with the packages he was carrying and Dawber's grumbling at his side, but he did it. They reached Dawber's lair, and up the stairs they went.

When at last Toby dropped his burdens, Dawber simply said, "Bath. Now."

Toby tipped his head. "Where, sir?"

Dawber rolled his eyes. "I left you alone up here

the other day. Any other boy would have known everything that was in this damned attic!"

He walked quickly over to the corner and pulled a large trunk away from the wall. And lo and behold, behind it stood a small cast-iron bathtub.

"Here," he said, pointing.

"Where's the water?" Toby asked, figuring that he'd have to haul it up from the street to the attic. He wasn't looking forward to it one bit.

But Dawber pointed to the ceiling. "Pipe," he said. "It's cold, but that will have to do."

Then he stepped around the tub, pulled a rusty chain that hung down, and which Toby hadn't noticed, and water gushed down into the tub, splashing out over the floorboards and surrounding crates.

"Not the best, but good enough, my dear," Dawber said, once the tub was full and he'd let go of the chain. Water continued to drip with slowing, echoing *plop*s.

"Bathe," Dawber said. "Now. Wash that hair, too. You'll find soap in the tub, and a washrag. Towels are over here." He pointed to the opposite side of the tub.

Toby asked, "Where's it drain to?"

Dawber rolled his eyes. "The alley, of course. And what do you care, my pretty? You're about to be a wealthy young man."

Dawber disappeared into his room, and Toby stripped down and settled into the tub. It wasn't as much of a shock to his system as he'd feared, for the water, which apparently was caught and stored up on the roof, was tepid instead of cold.

He scrubbed his hair twice and carefully washed all over, from behind his ears to between his toes. He didn't often have access to a real bath, and he secretly liked them. He liked getting wet, for one thing, and he liked the way he felt when he was well-scrubbed.

Why, if he had a tub of his own, he'd likely wash once a week—or more—without anybody to tell him!

And as he washed himself, he wondered if Bass had relayed his message to Fargo. He sure hoped so. And Bass would, if he could just keep it straight. That was the part that Toby was mostly worried about. Bass had a tendency to turn things around a little if he thought about them too much.

Once Toby had reluctantly hauled himself out of the cloudy but comfortable water, toweled off, and dressed in the new clothes Dawber had purchased—neat, but not too neat; pressed, but not too pressed—he called out, "Mr. Dawber? I'm ready, sir."

Still concerned about Cally, Fargo kept his eye peeled for even a glimpse of her as he made his way through the waterfront section, and up toward his hotel. As he left the poorer district, he began to catch the occasional sight of one of Dawber's boys, the ones he'd seen carrying in all that plunder when he'd watched the warehouse the other night.

One lad passed him casually, tucking a purse under his jacket, and he spied another in the act of picking the pocket of an elderly, well-dressed gentleman.

So this was why he hadn't seen the kids down on the riverfront! Dawber was smart, all right. He knew that the denizens of the docks had no money to steal. The money-bearing bodies were several streets up.

And this was where the boys plied their trade.

They did pretty well at it, too, from what Fargo had seen.

He walked a bit farther, and came to the Shea Hotel. He'd realized, as he walked, that he'd sent Bass Owen to hide—and await his twenty dollars—right in the room where he'd secreted his own stash of money.

Dumb, dumb, dumb.

Well, it couldn't be helped.

He'd lay anything that he was going to find a ransacked room and no kid. And no cash.

Damn it.

He got a spare key from the room clerk, climbed the stairs, and opened the door, prepared for the worst.

What he found was an untouched room—at first glimpse, anyhow—and Bass Owen, sound asleep on his mattress.

Despite himself, Fargo smiled. The poor little son of a gun. Dodging the police and sleeping in alleys could wear a boy down. In this case, at least, it certainly had.

Bass was dead to the world, and didn't wake when Fargo pulled out the bureau and untaped his cash from its back. Better safe than sorry, he thought, and let himself out. He left it in the hotel safe—a better place for it anyway, he told himself—then went back up.

Bass was still asleep, and just as well.

Fargo had a lot of thinking to do. He sat in the chair by the window and propped his head in his hand. What next?

He remembered the Beaufort case. The Beaufort's baby boy had been snatched, no ransom note was ever delivered, and the baby was presumed dead. As he recalled, that hadn't stopped everybody and his brother trying to get the reward. In fact, he remembered a newspaper article about how the Beaufort missing baby had accounted for a rash of kidnapped children in the area at the time.

All of them dark-haired, blue-eyed boys.

It seemed that Dawber had the same idea, even if it was a little late.

He turned his head back to glance at Bass. Hell, Fargo could probably try to pull the same trick with Bass, there, if he wasn't on the up and up. Fargo, that is. He wasn't yet certain where Bass stood on the more important moral issues.

Didn't matter, he supposed. Bass would do whatever it took to help out his buddy, and Fargo was counting on that. Just what it was he'd have to do though, remained to be seen.

He wondered. Should he take a little trip up to see Mr. and Mrs. Beaufort? If they still lived in St. Louis, that is. It had been a long time.

With his lips pursed and his eyes narrowed, he continued to think.

21

"So that's it," Emmy Beaufort said, staring, with eyes unfocused, at the nautical painting across the room. "And you planned to cross both of them."

"Actually, ma'am, I have already," Cally said. "By coming here, I mean."

"And I suppose you expect some sort of reward for this?"

Cally shook her head emphatically. "No, I don't want anything, Mrs. Beaufort, honest. I just don't want to see Dawber profit any more than he already has. Some things, a man just shouldn't take advantage of. Kids are one of them."

Emmy smiled. She stood up and went to the mantel. "And I suppose that old ladies are another?"

"Yes. I mean . . . oh shoot!"

When Emmy turned about, Cally was blushing furiously. "Don't worry about it, my dear," she said, amused at the girl's embarrassment but touched by it, too.

"Thank you ma'am," Cally said, staring at her shoes.

"I think," Emmy said thoughtfully as she gave a tug to the bell cord, "that perhaps you should stay here for a few days."

"But . . . but there's somebody I'll need to tell," Cally said. "If I'm gonna stay here, I mean. And you're awfully kind, Mrs. Beaufort."

"Call me Emmy."

Cally smiled. "Emmy, then. That's a pretty name. Short for Emily?"

"I'm afraid not," Emmy said kindly. "My father had a rather strange sense of female names. I was christened Encyclopedia, which my mother in her dismay then shortened to Emmy."

James rapped at the doors, and Emmy beckoned him in. She gave orders that he was to tell Cook that Miss Teach would be staying at the house—and taking all meals with them—until further notice, and that he should send one of the maids to freshen up the guest quarters.

"The green room, I think," she said, then turned to Cally. "It has such pleasant views, and a very comfortable mattress."

James bowed slightly. "Certainly, Madam."

"And when you've done all that," Emmy Beaufort continued, "you might send a message to that policeman you talked to this morning. Tell him that we will surely be needing him."

Cally gulped, and Emmy said, "Not to worry, my dear. You've done nothing wrong. I merely wish to put this monster, Dawber, away for as long as possible."

Cally nodded, and looked a little relieved.

"Will that be all, Madam?" James asked.

"Yes, thank you."

Bowing, James let himself from the room, leaving the two women alone again.

"I'm afraid, my dear," Emmy said, "that I don't feel you should leave the house for any reason, even to tell this friend of yours where you've gone. I'm sorry to be so dreary about it, but honestly, I think it's for your own safety. I wouldn't ask it if I didn't believe it was so."

Cally slumped a little, but said nothing.

Emmy sat down again, but this time reached her hands out, over her knees, and took Cally's fingers in hers. "It's a man you wish to tell, isn't it? Is it this Big Mike?"

"Oh, no!" Cally said emphatically. "It . . . it's somebody else. I'm through with Big Mike for good. I just want to get away, to get out of St. Louis. If I never see those docks again, it'll be too soon."

Emmy laughed softly and gave Cally's fingers a little squeeze, then let go and sat back. "This boy that Dawber's going to try to foist off on me. You have seen him, then?"

Cally bobbed her head. She was a charming little thing, Emmy thought, if you looked past the cheap and tawdry clothing. A good scrub, a decent milliner, and a trip to the dressmaker, and she could easily pass for society.

"I saw him, ma'am," Cally said. "I even talked to him. He's a real nice lad, if you ask me. When Dawber picked him up off the streets, that kid didn't have a clue. I mean, he's innocent in all this. He's an orphan, and for all he knows, you *could* be his true mama."

Emmy couldn't help herself. She supposed that hope never quit. She asked, "What does he look like, this lad? I mean, I assume he has the right coloring—dark hair and blue eyes—but what about the rest?"

Cally considered for a moment. "Well," she began, "he's tall. Taller then me by a bit. That's why I was surprised to see him up at Dawber's place. He looks a few years older than the rest of the boys. Dawber likes 'em best when they're ten or twelve. He said they can skinny through the crowds better that way. I mean, when they're small."

"Then he's tall," said Emmy. "Go on, my dear."

"Oh," Cally said, coloring slightly. It was quite fetching on her. "I'm sorry, Mrs. . . . I mean, I'm sorry, Emmy. Let's see. He has a cleft chin, I remember that. No dimples. Got kind of a squarish jaw, and eyes set all far apart, like. He's got kind of a dreamy look about him, like he's thinkin' about somethin' else half the time. He was real polite, too, as I recall. Always called everybody ma'am or sir. Always said thank you and please."

"And you say he was raised in an orphanage in Kansas City?"

Cally nodded again. "Yes ma'am. Least, that's what Big Mike told me. Toby said that he was left there, as a baby."

Emmy smoothed her skirts thoughtfully. "His eyes . . . Were they light or dark blue?"

"Dark," replied Cally. "Near black, as a matter of fact. Indigo, I'd say. Why?"

"No reason," Emmy answered. But her darling Teddy's eyes had been dark blue, as blue as a thunderstorm, as blue as the deep blue sea.

Hope could be a dangerous thing.

Big Mike, after hiking to the place where Skinny last saw Cally, had turned Skinny loose, and had kept on walking alone.

But he could turn up neither hide nor hair of her. He cursed her in her absence, shouted at her, and even punched a lamppost. But all it did was hurt his hand.

Dammit, didn't she know that Dawber could move on his plan at any time? That he could take the kid up there and cut them clear out of the deal?

Course, that was more like keeping them from cutting Dawber out . . .

Hell. One thing was the same as the other to Big Mike. All he saw at the moment was that Cally had crossed him, crossed both Dawber and him. And he didn't like it, not one bit.

He stood there, next to the lamppost, rubbing his bruised knuckles, and decided to go back down and check the Little Cougar again. Hell, she might have come back. She'd *better* have.

And if not, well, then he'd just have to take care of both of them himself.

The thought gave him an unaccustomed chill. Not Cally, of course. Her tiny neck could be wrung as easy as he'd throttle a chicken. But Dawber? True, Mike had perhaps a hundred pounds on the little weasel. Big Mike was a fighter and a brawler by nature, and Dawber was a talker and a thinker.

But he'd seen the things that Dawber was capable of when you pushed him up against a hard place.

And they weren't pretty.

They even gave Big Mike the willies.

Whatever he did would have to be quick, he thought as he walked back down to the docks. Quick and clean. He'd have to kill Dawber outright.

If he only wounded Dawber, it'd likely be the last thing he ever did.

Fargo woke Bass. It was almost dark, and he'd let him sleep as long as he dared. He had business to take care of, and he didn't figure to leave Bass alone in his room while he took care of it. He wasn't too keen on the idea, but Bass was coming along.

"What?" said Bass, one eye slitted open.

"Come on," said Fargo. "We've got some business to see to."

"What business?"

"Saving your friend, Toby," said Fargo. "That good enough for you?"

The kid was up like a shot, and Fargo had to give him credit.

"Where're we goin'," he asked groggily as he tugged his boots on.

"We're going to the police station, and then, if we're lucky, we're going on a little raid," Fargo said.

"What's a raid?" Bass said as they went through the door.

"You'll find out."

Detective Sergeant G. G. Rawlings sat behind his desk, chewing his cigar, and listening to James Donovan, butler to Mrs. Wallings Beaufort, tell his tale of woe.

Actually, it wasn't so much a tale of woe as it was

a call for help, James thought. And immediate help at that.

"I am telling you, sir," he said, "that we need assistance as soon as possible. Couldn't you spare a couple of men to—"

Rawlings shook his head. "From what you're telling me, you got no idea when Dawber's gonna show up, or even if he's gonna show at all." He sat forward in his chair. "Now, I'm not fooling when I tell you that we'd like to get Dawber. Like to take him off the streets once and for all. But he's slippery, that one. He's not likely to make a move if he sees a couple of my boys hangin' about. This ain't like the old days when we could just go pick up somebody and hang 'em on general suspicion. Now they've got rules and courts an such," he said, as if longing for the old days.

"You're telling me that you're not going to do a blessed thing, aren't you?" James asked, slowly grinding his teeth.

"About the size of it," said Rawlings. " 'Less, of course, he actually shows up and demands payment for the kid. Then we could maybe step in. But Mrs. Beaufort has some kind of a standing reward as I hear it. Right?"

"Correct," James replied. He had thought it was a bad idea, but then, it wasn't his place to make comments or criticisms. "A standing reward of ten thousand."

Rawlings's brows shot up. "Jesus! Dollars?"

James nodded. "I believe so, sir," he said dryly.

"Turds," the detective mumbled. Then he spoke up again. "Well, nothin' we can do at all, then. Got to catch him bamboozlin' her, gotta catch him in the act, and she's made that just about impossible. See, the way the law looks at it, Dawber could have the kid. I mean, the real one. He could be demandin' his just rewards. Not that it's likely, but it's the law."

James scraped back his chair and stood stiffly. "Very well, then," he said. "And thank you for all your help." He didn't mean it in the slightest. "We shall call you if we need you."

As James left the police station, he nearly collided with an ill-dressed man with a beard, followed by a ragtag, dark-haired lad.

"Pardon me," he said, out of habit.

The bearded man shouted, "No problem," over his shoulder, and the two hurried up the steps.

James settled his hat on his head as Max pulled the buggy up. He got in.

22

"Well, that's different!" exclaimed Detective Sergeant Rawlings and jumped to his feet.

This action startled young Bass, who practically fell out of his chair. It sort of surprised Fargo, too.

"What do you mean, different?" Fargo asked. His brow furrowed. "Has somebody been in here before us? Somebody about Dawber, I mean?"

"Hell, yeah," said Rawlings, pulling on his jacket. "But that was just some butler from up on the hill, complainin' about some con job he thought Dawber was gonna pull on his employer. Can't do nothin' about that till it happens, you know? But this, this is great news! You found the hiding place! Why, we can nab him and all his rotten kids now! Gotta get him with evidence, and them kids—and his stash of loot, if he's got any and I'll bet he has—is evidence."

Rawlings started for the door.

Fargo reached out a hand and stopped him. "That wasn't Mrs. Wallings Beaufort's butler, was it?"

Rawlings stopped in his tracks, and his bulldog face darkened. "How the hell'd you know that?" And then, without waiting for an answer, he said, "C'mon. You can tell me on the way." He stepped into the outer office and shouted, "Hey, Clifford! Round up about ten men, and in a hurry. We're gonna bust that old bastard Dawber in his den tonight!"

* * *

Big Mike, having had no luck finding Cally, took it upon himself to at last wander up to the Beaufort mansion.

He'd been hanging around across the street, behind a tall hedge of lilacs, for the last two hours, trying to decide whether to go and ring the bell or not. He sure couldn't see any sign of Cally from out here, but then, how could he? And nobody had left or gone away since he'd been here.

He heard a carriage coming up the bricked street, and crouched down so the bushes would hide him completely. But the carriage didn't pass. Instead, it turned into the Beaufort drive and continued on around to the back.

There was nobody in it but the driver up top and a tall, skinny man in the passenger seat, both of whom he automatically filed away as being no threat. He could smash the two of them with one blow.

But if that gent had been out someplace, it might have been to meet Cally. Skinny had said she took off with a feller at about noon. Course, Skinny didn't say anything about a carriage or a driver, but then, maybe that part had happened later. And even Big Mike, who wasn't the sharpest tool in the shed, couldn't imagine that Cally being with somebody from the Beaufort's place was a coincidence.

"Just what the hell's goin' on here?" he muttered to himself, and swatted at a bee.

More swiftly than Fargo had imagined the police could move, Rawlings's men thundered down to the dock district, stopped about two blocks away from Dawber's lair, and left the wagons and buggies behind.

They split up into twos and threes, and came at the old warehouse from several sides at once. Fargo wasn't allowed to go in with the first group, although he complained heartily. But when an officer sounded the all clear, he and Bass and Detective Rawlings tore up the unsteady staircases and hurried to the attic.

About a dozen and a half boys were being taken

into custody. Policemen were rifling Dawber's room and coming up with all sorts of goodies the man had hidden away, but there was no sign of Dawber. Or Toby.

Fargo stuck his head into Dawber's room, where one policeman was sitting on the bed and holding up a string of pearls, a look of amazement on his face. A second policeman was just pulling another stash out from beneath a crate.

"You find a red ruby ring in there," Fargo said, "it belongs to a friend of mine. Armstrong Leery. Got that?"

"Got it," said the first policeman, never taking his eyes off the pearls.

The second policeman glanced toward Fargo. "We'll keep an eye open for it, sir."

Detective Rawlings walked up behind Fargo and tapped him on the shoulder. "Well, no Dawber."

"And my kid's not here, either," Fargo replied.

"Your kid?"

Fargo sighed. "The kid I was lookin' for. The one Dawber's trying to foist off on Mrs. Beaufort. Listen, Rawlings, if you've got any brain left in that head of yours, you'll get a bunch of these men over to the Beaufort place, because I'll bet you anything that's where you'll find Dawber."

Rawlings stood there a moment, chewing on his cigar. "Hell," he said. "You know these kids ain't gonna give him up, Fargo or Drinkwater or whatever your name is."

"It's Fargo."

"Fine."

"But stop and consider, Rawlings," Fargo said. "If these kids knew that Dawber was in custody, they might sing a different tune. Toby would, for certain."

"Yes sir," piped up Bass, who had been riveted on the scene around him. "It ain't right, what this Dawber was doin' to these boys. And Toby's a stand-up sort of cuss. They ain't gonna be in any trouble are they?"

Rawlings tousled the boy's hair. "Not too much, Bass. We'll process 'em, then try to get 'em out into foster care. Or over to the orphanage."

"Oh," said Bass, not bothering to mask his distaste. He must not think much of orphanages, Fargo thought, and probably with good reason.

"Well, I'm going to the Beaufort place, whether you're coming or not," Fargo announced to Rawlings, and started for the doorway.

"Hold on, there," said Rawlings, and took the cigar out of his mouth. "Clifford!" he shouted. "You up here?"

A lean man with reddish hair and a large mustache looked up from his clipboard and shouted, "Here, boss!"

Rawlings said, "You take over here. Briggs and Hartley, come with us."

It was just past dusk and Big Mike was still in the bushes when a hansom cab pulled up to the Beaufort home. Dawber climbed down, along with Toby, and Big Mike was suddenly at attention.

"You double-crossin' son of a bitch!" Mike growled under his breath, and unconsciously balled his hands into big, meaty fists.

"First that goddamn Cally runs off, and now this," he grumbled as they paid the driver, and the cab clopped away, up the street. And as he watched them travel up the long walk to the front porch, anger rose up in him, clouding his reason.

"The hell with this crud," he said, and emerged from the hedge. Lilacs from the shrubbery trailed and dropped from his shirt and trousers as he made for the Beaufort's front door, which was just then closing behind Dawber and the kid.

"Hey!" said Bass suddenly, and twisted around in the wagon to face Fargo. "It just hit me. You ain't . . . you ain't any kin to that Fargo in the books, are you?"

He had to shout, because the police wagon in which they were riding was barreling along the streets at top speed. Fargo clung to the seat and hoped for the best. He wished he was on the Ovaro, and he wished there was nothing but open plain between where they were and the Beaufort place. He'd lost his city hat blocks ago.

And he wished they were moving faster.

"Not kin," he shouted back to Bass. He didn't feel like explaining at the moment. And then, to the wagon's driver, he yelled, "Can't you get any more speed outta that team?"

Beside him, Rawlings was also braced for the worst, clinging to both the armrest and the seat in front of him. His hat was off and clamped under his armpit. The cigar still jutted from his mouth, though.

Around it, Rawlings shouted, "He's doin' the best he can in this traffic, Fargo." And then, jaws clenched, he shouted to the officer at the reins, "Goddamn it, Briggs! Move this thing!"

"I see," said Emmy Beaufort after Dawber had explained, with exceeding politeness and gentility—and lies, lies, lies—who he thought the boy beside him on the sofa to be.

"You are surely a handsome lad, and you do favor my late husband," she said, not daring to hope. This boy, this beautiful boy, might be her Teddy. He even had her Wallings's eyes. She told herself *no, don't be silly,* and said, "But of course, we will have to do some checking. I'm sure you understand."

Dawber opened his mouth to answer, but before he could there came a thunderous crash from the hall outside, and then the study doors ripped from their rails and crashed inward.

Emmy shot to her feet and crossly said, "Those were pocket doors, you fool!" before she knew what she was doing. And also before she realized how enormous the door-smasher was.

He was a mountain, Paul Bunyan incarnate, except that he looked very, very cross. And he didn't have a blue ox with him.

"Dawber!" he barked, ignoring her completely. "You crossed me, you poisonous bastard! And what'd you do with Cally, kill her? She's my goddamn meal ticket!"

He pulled out an enormous knife and started forward.

And at that precise moment, Emmy Beaufort fainted.

Cally, who had heard Big Mike's furious roar, snuck down the back steps. She was just turning for the servant's entrance when she saw the poor butler lying in the main hall in a pool of blood, and went to him despite her trembling. Like a child who cannot help but go to the aid of an injured puppy, she was helpless to stop herself, even in the face of possible discovery by Big Mike.

She crept past the battered-down study doors to the downed butler and knelt beside him. She touched his face gently and said, "James?"

Now Dawber was shouting, too, and somebody was breaking the furniture.

"James!" she hissed.

And his eyes fluttered. He looked up at her—how miraculous that he was still alive!—and whispered, "Get help, Miss. Now. I shall be all right."

She scrambled to her feet, slipped in the blood that was still seeping from his head, caught herself on a side table, and dashed for the front door.

Someone howled in rage and pain behind her, but she didn't stop. She yanked the door open.

And ran straight into Drinkwater's arms.

"In there, Drinkwater!" she shouted, pointing to the source of the racket. "In there!"

It wasn't until he'd gone past her that she realized there were other people with him, uniformed policemen among them.

23

Fargo leapt over the butler's prone body and barely noticed that Rawlings shouted, "Briggs! Take care of him!"

He was rushing toward the noise. Which stopped just before he reached the study.

A woman—Mrs. Beaufort, he supposed—lay on the floor, and Toby was headed for her, a look of concern on his face. Big Mike, twisted in death, rested on top of a broken tea table. Fargo was boggled that Dawber could have taken him out. "How?" he asked.

"Ice pick," Toby said in a quavering, breaking voice. The boy was now kneeling beside Mrs. Beaufort, patting her limp hand. "It just came outta nowhere . . ."

"Where's Dawber, goddamn it?" thundered Rawlings.

"T-there," stuttered Toby, and pointed toward the room's service door.

Fargo was through it like a shot.

He ran through the house to the kitchen, where a fat woman in a white uniform was cowering in the corner.

"Where?" Fargo shouted.

The woman lifted a shaking hand and pointed to the back door.

Once out on the wide rear porch, he saw just a

glimpse of a man's coat flick out of sight, behind the corner of a house not three lots away. Dawber.

Fargo took the stairs in four steps and began running over turf, through bushes, under trees. He leapt fences and hopped over and around decorative statuary, sometimes losing sight of Dawber, sometimes keeping him in sight for seconds at a time.

Panting hard, Fargo chased him down, down toward the river, and as he ran, he wondered if Dawber was out of breath, too, or if Dawber was some kind of freak superior physical specimen. He'd killed Big Mike, after all.

But Fargo was so intent on catching up to him that he brushed aside these misgivings. He just ran.

They were on the city streets, now, running through downtown St. Louis, or its periphery, and now Fargo could see his quarry for blocks at a time. They both darted through pedestrian crowds, and Fargo leapt over the people Dawber knocked down.

If Rawlings or one of his men had been on Fargo's tail, they'd long since dropped by the wayside. He grimaced, expecting an ambush each time he followed Dawber around a sharp turn into an alley, but Dawber was never there. He was always ahead, running, running.

At one point, Dawber, a block and a half ahead of him, turned and shook his fist, then took off again. Fargo didn't know how the man kept it up! Now, Fargo himself was a horseman, unaccustomed to walking, let alone running, and it was taking its toll. But he figured that he was at least twenty or thirty years younger than Dawber. The man's stamina was amazing.

Both Dawber and Fargo were down to a jog now, but neither of them gave up. They ran past Fargo's hotel, and as they did, he had a crazy idea.

He whistled just as loud as his aching lungs would allow as he neared the livery where he'd left the Ovaro. He knew the horse was loose in a box stall, but wasn't sure whether he could break down the stall door. Still, he was desperate. He whistled again, the loud, long, high-pitched blast that both he and the horse knew meant *come here, and come right now*.

As he neared the stable, he gave up hope. There was a ruckus coming from the stable, all right, but no horse. Still, he whistled again. It was all he could manage.

Just as he lost sight of Dawber again, and had run past the door of the stable, not daring to take precious seconds to go in and retrieve his mount, he heard hooves thundering behind him. He turned to see the welcome sight of the Ovaro, wearing nothing but a halter and bleeding from a long jagged scratch down his neck.

Whirling about, Fargo grasped a hunk of the stallion's mane and swung himself up onto the Ovaro's back.

He sank his heels into the horse.

Using his body weight and touches on the horse's neck, he galloped down the block and into an alley. Dawber's coat was just disappearing around the next corner.

Bending low over the horse's neck, he cornered sharply, caught up with Dawber in a flash, and leapt, catlike, from the stallion's back onto the shoulders of the running man.

Dawber went skidding down to the bricks, and Fargo went with him. The bricks took the cloth of his sleeve and shredded it, along with some skin, but Fargo barely noticed, for Dawber suddenly wrenched violently and turned himself over, flinging Fargo flat into a brick wall.

He landed with a resounding "Oof!" just in time to see Dawber gain his feet once more and take off across the street, into a large building.

Glancing down the street to see if the Ovaro had stopped—he had, about a block away—Fargo darted after Dawber.

The building was some sort of office, and he followed Dawber's trail by the straggling employees he'd knocked over on his way. Up the stairs Fargo chased him, hearing the thuds of his scurrying boot steps, always just out of reach.

Up he went, until he was on the roof. Dawber was at the edge, just climbing down to hop to the next roof, a story below. He dropped, but Fargo didn't take time to judge the jump. He just barreled after Dawber and took a literal leap of faith.

And on his arcing, free-falling path downward, his boot hit Dawber in the head.

Fargo landed on his hands and knees. Dawber hit the roof on his back, cracking his head audibly.

But still, the bastard got up! He glared at Fargo, and breathlessly said, "Well, now. Drinkwater. What are you, really? St. Louis police? Pinkerton?"

Fargo jacked the derringer down what was left of his sleeve. He huffed, "Just the friend of a man who lost a ruby ring to your kids. Come on. Hands on top of your head."

But Dawber made no move to comply. Hands on his knees, he panted, "I understand those are a very poor weapon. Very difficult to aim. Very unreliable, old sport."

"Hands up," Fargo repeated. "Now."

"I don't think so," said Dawber. He immediately turned and ran toward the roofline.

Fargo fired.

The shot took Dawber in the thigh. He stumbled, then recovered himself. Fargo heard him mumble something, but he couldn't tell what.

Fargo shouted, "Stop now, Dawber."

But Dawber didn't. Never looking back at Fargo, he moved toward the roofline again.

Fargo fired his second and last shot, and prayed the gun would shoot truer this time.

This time, his slug took Dawber in the back. Dawber stopped, wavering near the edge of the roof for what seemed like forever, and then he fell forward. He dropped out of sight.

Fargo heard him hit the street below. It sounded a little like a ripe melon thrown from a barn roof.

Still huffing, Fargo followed and sat down, hard, on the edge of the roof. Below him, a crowd was slowly gathering. Dawber lay two stories beneath him in a slowly spreading pool of blood.

And Fargo? He felt damned good about it. And he was by God going to good and well catch his breath before he went down to retrieve the body.

"They said at the hotel that I might find you here," said a voice behind him in the stable.

Fargo turned around, the Ovaro's jar of salve still in his hand, to see the morning sun beaming in behind Cally. She was carrying a fat satchel.

Fargo spread a last line of the ointment over the Ovaro's neck scratch, then patted him on the forehead. It had been superficial, but the damage to the stall had set him back fifteen dollars.

"Mornin', Cally," he said, letting himself out of the stall. "You bring Toby and his pardner with you?"

Cally smiled. "No. You never did get back to the house last night, did you?"

Fargo latched the stall door and set the ointment aside. Cally looked awful pretty in this light. Of course, she looked pretty good in any light—or no light at all, come to think of it.

He said, "Where is Toby, then? The police station?"

"No," Cally said, and set down her valise. "He's up at the Beaufort house. Along with his friend, Bass Owen. Mrs. Beaufort's taking them in, bless her heart."

Fargo's eyebrows shot up. "She is?"

"Cross my heart, and hope to die," Cally said with a grin. "She's a real pip, that one. She said she'd been waiting long enough, searching long enough. She said she'd like two boys instead of one to help make up for lost time."

Fargo scratched his head. "Well, I'll be double-dogged."

"And she's taking care of those other boys, too," Cally went on. "That's my new job. She's buyin' a big house just up the street from where she lives. The Wallings Beaufort Institute for Lost Youth, she's gonna call it. And I'm gonna help to run it. Me! Can you imagine?"

It had been a long time since he'd heard such good news. He moved toward her and took her in his arms. "That I can Cally. That I can. When do you have to report?"

She laughed. "It doesn't matter. You thinkin' what I'm thinkin'?"

"Exactly what you're thinking, Cally mine. I just happen to have a morning to spare, myself. I can't pick up Armstrong's ring at the station until after two."

"Who's Armstrong?" she said, as arm in arm they walked from the stable and started toward his hotel.

"Doesn't matter," he said, raising her bag to carry it under his other arm. It was heavy. *She must have everything she owns in here, and an anvil, too,* he thought.

They turned in at the hotel entrance, and Fargo helped her up the stairs.

"Sorry," she said as he unlocked his room door.

"Sorry?" he asked. "What for?"

She stepped inside. "You told me the truth. You really are Fargo. *That* Fargo. I shouldn't have made fun of you."

He locked the door behind him, and put her satchel on the floor. The light streamed through his window, glittering gold with dust motes, and ended on his coverlet.

He laid a tender hand on her shoulder. "That man in the books? You're right. He's made up."

"But based on the truth," she said as he began to unbutton her blouse.

"Just based," he said. He smiled. "Then it wanders a good bit."

"Like you," she said, and began to untie the strings on his britches. "I like your buckskins. They're sorta wildlike."

He slid the blouse off her shoulders. "You don't mind about Big Mike?"

She shrugged. "Thought I would. I really did. But when I saw him lyin' there, I was just . . . relieved, I guess."

"Good," he whispered, and eased the straps of her camisole from her shoulders to bare those beautiful breasts.

"Fargo?" she murmured.

"Yes, Cally?"

"Are we gonna talk all day, or are you going to make love to me?"

Grinning, he pushed her back on the bed, then, laughing, fell atop of her.

LOOKING FORWARD!

**The following is the opening
section of the next novel in the exciting
Trailsman series from Signet:**

**THE TRAILSMAN #272
NEVADA NEMESIS**

The big man in buckskins caught up with the wagon
train a week after he struck its trail. From a rise, Skye
Fargo watched the nine wagons plod southwest across
the alkali flats like so many canvas-backed turtles. A
thick cloud of dust moved with them, shimmering in
the heat haze.

Nevada Territory was like that. Hot and dusty and
sparse on vegetation. An iron land, unrelenting and
cruel, home to the hardiest of animals and some of
the cruelest of men. It was no place for pilgrims bound
for the promised land of milk and honey. Yet there
they were.

Fargo's lake-blue eyes narrowed. He had spotted
two outriders well ahead of the wagons. They were
the only ones on horseback. Gigging his Ovaro down
the slope, he matched their snail's pace. It would be
dark in a couple of hours. That was when he would
make their acquaintance.

Both Fargo and the Ovaro were caked with dust.

His white hat was brown with it. He inhaled it when he breathed and tasted it when he swallowed. He wryly reflected that if dust ever became valuable, the few folks living in Nevada would be downright rich.

In the distance reared one of the more than thirty mountain ranges that slashed the territory from north to south. It didn't have an official name yet, to the best of Fargo's knowledge, although the old-timers sometimes referred to it as the Blood Red Range, after the crimson snow plants that pushed through the snow in the forests at the higher elevations.

A few prospectors had searched its peaks over the years but none ever struck it rich. The Northern Paiutes and the Western Shoshones both roamed the region. They were on peaceful terms with whites at the moment, although the army had received a recent report of a band of young Paiutes making trouble.

The piercing cry of a hawk drew Fargo's gaze to the sky. Other than lizards and snakes and rabbits, wildlife was scarce. He had heard coyotes yipping the night before. But he had not seen any sign of bears, wolves, or deer since leaving the vicinity of the Snake River.

Fargo figured he was far enough back that he would go unnoticed by the emigrants. Then a shout arose from the last wagon and was relayed up the line. Soon the pair of outriders were galloping to intercept him. As they came up he studied them from under his hat brim, and he did not like what he saw.

The rider on the right was as stout as a barrel and as greasy as bear fat. A Remington was strapped around his waist, and the hilt of a knife jutted from the top of his right boot.

The rider on the left was a runt with a chin that jutted like a lance tip and a nose shaped like a fishhook. He wore a Smith and Wesson. On his head was a raccoon hat that had seen better days.

Neither had taken a bath in a month of Sundays.

They were filthy, their clothes were filthy, their saddles were filthy. They reined up twenty feet away and the stout one raised his hand. "Hold it right there, mister."

Fargo kept riding slowly toward them. He had the reins in his left hand and his right hand on his hip, inches from his Colt.

"Didn't you hear Swink?" the runt barked. "He told you to halt and you'd damned well better listen."

Fargo did not say anything. Nor did he stop. He focused on their gun hands, waiting for a telltale twitch or the jerk of an elbow.

Swink reined his horse so it was directly in the Ovaro's path. "By God, you'll do as we say. Ain't that right, Raskum?"

"It sure is," the runt echoed.

The Ovaro was only a few feet from Swink's sorrel when Fargo drew rein. "Move," he said.

Swink and Raskum looked at one another and Swink responded, "Is your brain sunbaked? You're not going anywhere until you tell us who you are and what you're doing here."

"We're the pilots for those prairie schooners yonder," Raskum added, "and we don't want you near them."

Fargo leaned on his saddle horn. He had worked as a pilot on occasion, and he knew many of the professional pilots who made their livings guiding wagon trains from Independence, Missouri to Oregon Country or California. He had never seen these two before. "I'm not contagious."

"Huh?" Raskum said. "What the hell does a disease have to do with anything? We don't care if you've got the measles."

"He means there's no reason for us to keep him from going near the others," Swink explained.

"We don't need a reason," Raskum said. "We're

the pilots. We can do whatever we damn well feel like."

Fargo reined to the right and started to go around them. For a few moments they were speechless with surprise, then both reined their mounts and came up on either side of his pinto stallion.

"Mister, you must have rocks between your ears," Raskum snapped. "If you don't stop that nag right this second, I'm liable to wallop you over the head with the butt of my pistol."

"That's a good idea," Fargo said. His Colt was in his hand before either could think to stop him. He slammed the butt against Raskum's temple and the runt keeled from the saddle like a whiskey-soaked drunk and struck the ground with a thud. Spinning the Colt, Fargo pointed it at Swink. "Your turn. Unless you're more reasonable than your pard."

Swink's Adam's apple was bobbing up and down like a walnut on a wind-tossed branch. "Me? Hell. Reasonable is my middle name. If you want to join us a spell, go right ahead. But you can't blame us for being cautious. It's our job to make sure those people don't come to harm."

Fargo twirled the Colt into his holster. "You boys should pick a new line of work. You're not much good at this one." He rode on.

Swink quickly caught up. "You're mighty slick on the draw, stranger. Mighty slick. I never saw your hand move. Not many men are that fast. I don't suppose you're someone I might have heard of?"

Fargo changed the subject. "Are you just going to leave your friend back there?"

"Hell, I've wanted to thump him on the head a few times myself to stop him from flappin' his gums. He can jabber rings around a tree."

"One of those," Fargo said to keep him talking. The pair matched the description he had been given but they were only the first link in the chain.

"Sometimes we can't be too choosy about who we partner up with," Swink commented. "And Raskum has his good points. He makes the best coffee this side of St. Louis, and he doesn't snore." Swink paused. "Do you have a handle or would that be prying?"

"I have a handle and it would be prying."

"Fair enough. Never let it be said I can't take a hint." He took the hint for all of ten seconds. "What are you doing in these parts? There isn't a town within hundreds of miles."

"I had to leave Salt Lake in a hurry," Fargo said. Which wasn't true. But he could hardly admit the real reason he was there.

Swink grinned. "I savvy. Don't worry. Your secret is safe with me. I've ridden a few high lines in my time and I know what it's like to have the law breathin' down your neck."

"And now you're a wagon train pilot?" Fargo tried to keep the skepticism out of his voice.

"Heh. Let's just say things aren't always what we think they are and let it go at that." Swink looked back. Raskum was still serving as a fly stool. "Damn. I hope he ain't dead. I don't want to take these lunkheads the rest of the way by my lonesome."

The Conestogas had come to a stop. Men, women, and children were leaning from their seats or peering from the back of the wagons. A curly-mopped girl of seven or eight smiled and waved in greeting.

The drivers of the first two prairie schooners had climbed down and were waiting with rifles cradled in the crooks of their arms. One was almost as broad-shouldered as Fargo and wore clothes typical of a farmer: overalls, homespun shirt, and a short-brimmed hat. He was close to forty, his arms thick with muscle. The second driver wasn't more than twenty. Lean and gangly, he also bore the stamp of a tiller of the soil. A corncob pipe jutted from his shirt pocket.

The bigger man started right in. "Mr. Swink, who

is this stranger and why have you brought him among us after what he did to Mr. Raskum?"

Fargo answered before Swink could. "He doesn't have any say in the matter. I do what I want when I want."

"Now see here." The big farmer gripped his Sharps in both brawny hands. "I'm the leader here, and I do have a say in things."

"No, you don't." Fargo swung down and walked to a water barrel on the second wagon. Without asking permission he opened it, lowered the dipper in, and treated himself to a swallow.

"That's my water," the young farmer said.

"*Our* water," someone corrected him, and a young woman swung from the seat and put her hands on her hips and glared at Fargo. She had fine blond hair done up in a bun and blue eyes that flashed with anger. "And I'll thank you, whoever you are, not to drink any without our permission."

Fargo took another swallow while admiring the swell of her bosom and the flair of her thighs. "The name is Flint."

"Well, Mr. Flint, you have some gall riding in here like this," the woman declared. "If you're not careful, we'll send you packing."

"You're welcome to try." Fargo gazed the length of the wagon train. The little girl in the last wagon waved again. "You folks sure are off the beaten path."

"We're taking a shortcut—," the young man began, and was immediately hushed by the older one.

"It's unwise to confide our personal affairs, Jared. We want no part of Mr. Flint and bid him to move on."

"Do you have a name or should I just call you stupid?" Fargo asked.

The big farmer drew himself up to his full height. "I'm Peter Sloane, of the Iowa Sloanes. Our family has been in this country since seventeen ninety-six.

My grandfather came over from Belgium and was one of the first farmers in Appanoose County."

Fargo gave the dipper to the blonde. Her nostrils flared and she hefted it as if she were contemplating hitting him. "Maybe you should have stayed there. Where you're headed, there's no law and little water."

"Our pilots know every creek and water hole in these parts," Sloane said. "As for the other, we have plenty of guns." He patted his Sharps. "No hostiles or owl hoots would dare tangle with us."

Fargo could point out that their train was much too small for there to be any safety in their numbers. He could also point out that nearly every creek was dry at that time of the year and water holes were few and far between. But all he said was, "Some lessons are only learned the hard way."

"You'll be moving on now that you've had a drink?" Swink asked hopefully.

Fargo shook his head. "I'm going to keep these fine folks company a while." He stepped to the Ovaro to climb back on and spotted Raskum galloping madly toward them.

Peter Sloane's cheeks had flushed and his knuckles grew white on the Sharps. "Now see here, Mr. Flint. We decide who can and can't join us. It's in the agreement each of us signed."

"I never signed it," Fargo said, placing his right hand on his Colt and his left hand on his saddle.

"Need I point out that you are only one man?" Sloane said smugly. "I daresay you will do as we want or suffer the consequences."

In a thundering cloud of dust Raskum drew rein and sprang to the ground. "You!" he roared at Fargo, glowering pure hate. "My head is splittin' because of what you did!"

"Look at the bright side," Fargo said. "You're still breathing."

Raskum's hand hovered over his Smith and Wesson. "No one does that to me! Do you hear?"

"You brought it on yourself." Fargo glanced from the runt to Swink and back again. Swink showed no inclination to lend his friend a hand. "But if you want to die, I'll oblige you."

Peter Sloane moved toward Raskum but stopped when Raskum shot him a savage glare. "I ask you to reconsider, pilot. This is no place for gunplay. Women and children are present."

"What do you know, you stupid potato planter?" Raskum spat. Any self-restraint he had was gone. "Out here a man has to stick up for himself or he's branded no-account. This peckerwood put a welt on me the size of a hen's egg and he has to answer for it."

Fargo had a decision to make. He would just as soon put a slug between Raskum's ears and be done with it, but the army was counting on him. Lives were at stake. Not just those of Sloane and his people, but those of emigrants who might come along the Oregon Trail next month or next year or the year after. Raskum was still glaring at Peter Sloane, so he took a quick step and planted his boot in the runt's groin.

Gurgling and grunting, Raskum clutched himself and tottered. "You—you—you—," he huffed.

Fargo slugged him on the jaw and Raskum sprawled face first in the dust and didn't move.

The farmers were rooted in shock. Peter Sloane's mouth opened and closed a few times but no words came out.

Bending, Fargo relieved Raskum of the Smith and Wesson and tossed it to Swink. "Hold on to this. Your friend will live longer without it."

Jared was in awe. "You whipped him without half trying."

"Violence is the last resort of the godless," Peter Sloane piously intoned. "Mr. Flint, you will leave, and you will leave this instant, or I will call all the men together and we will thrash you soundly."

Fargo stepped into the stirrups. "If anyone so much as lifts a finger against me, you'll be burying a lot of your own. Let's get going. There's still a lot of daylight left."

The blonde was fit to spit nails. "What do we do, Mr. Sloane? We can't let him boss us around like this."

"I'm afraid, Miss Fox, that for the time being we have no choice," Peter Sloane said. "This man is coming with us whether we like it or not."

Which was exactly what Fargo wanted to hear.